Arm in Arm

With

The Holy Spirit

Patrick Day

Pyramid Publishers

1314 Grandview Circle

Buffalo, MN 55313

763-486-2867

www.pyramidpublishers.com

Second Edition

Printed by Lightning Source 1246 Heil Quaker Blvd. La Vergne, TN USA 37086
ISBN – 978-0-9851514-6-1

Cover Design by Myron Sahlberg
Interior Design by Just Ink Digital Design
Printed in the United States of America

Prologue

You are the song in me today,
With all I think and all I say,
With all events that come my way.

Your melody my spirit plays;
I'll tune within and humbly praise
Your presence in me all my days.

It's not what I achieve for You;
I'll strive no more in all I do.
It's only what You do through me;
I'll wait for You on bended knee.

AUTHOR'S NOTE

I use the term "more of God" often throughout this story and want to explain with precision what I mean. "More of God" is relative to the inner being of a believer, not a description of God Himself. It is what John the Baptist means when he says, "He must become greater; I must become less."

We cannot measure God in terms of pints, bushels, or even oceans. All of Him is in the spirit of a Christian and fully available from the day of salvation. But we don't always draw on the power of God; too often we go our own way or the way of the world. My definition of "more of God" is to have more of Him in our mind, will, and emotions, not more of Him in our spirits.

There is either more of God or more of ourselves and the world at any given point in time. This more of God may happen in our lives some of the time, more of the time, or most of the time. It should be our goal to arrive at the place where we experience more of God most of the time.

More of God means more reading Scripture and more listening for the Holy Spirit. It means following Jesus every step of the way, including more prayer and more awareness of Him in our everyday lives. The first three requests in the Lord's Prayer are a good summary of this moreness:

- more hallowing of His name
- more becoming involved in His kingdom here on earth and His kingdom yet to come.
- more bending our will to His.

More of God is the extent to which the Holy Spirit moves us if we allow Him to do so – some of the time, more of the time, or most of the time.

MORE OF GOD SOME OF THE TIME

1

Friday, October 14, 2011. My name is Paul Chambers, or at least I think it is. Right now I'm not sure of anything. I am sitting in my home office with my outside jacket still on, clutching the sides of my roll-top desk. My eyes are burning and tears are furrowing down my cheeks. In my imagination I see a lifelike scene of a deep, dark pit beneath my feet. A sinister figure is trying to push me into it and I'm terrified. My shirt is drenched with sweat and small droplets are falling from my whiskers. I don't know which way is up.

An hour ago a doctor told me I have pancreatic cancer and less than a year to live. I sat in stunned silence, gasping for breath. My wife, Molly, fainted and fell to the floor. It took ten minutes to revive her.

I left the doctor's office leading Molly as if she were blind and in a trance. I don't know how we made it home. The car must have been on autopilot. My emotions were strained and swirling, vacillating between fear and anger. I think I was at a stoplight when I shouted out: "How can it be, Lord? I have a new cancer just as the other one is in remission?" The people in the car next to me looked over. Did they hear what I had just said? In a softer voice I lamented, "This is like getting out of the hospital from a bad car accident and being run over by a hearse on the way home."

Molly heard none of what I said. When we arrived home, she immediately went to the couch in the living room and remained there like a dead person sitting up. I didn't know how to help her; my state of being was not that far removed from hers. I stumbled into my office and trembled at my desk, distraught and barely in touch with reality, the dark pit beneath my feet waiting for me to become part of it.

After several minutes, I let go of the desk and stared out my office window. The anger has subsided, replaced by a cheerless calm. The leaves are starting to fall and decay, and soon I will be with them. In a soft whisper I ask, "Where are You now, Lord? How will I get through this?" Thoughts flutter through my mind like leaves turning in the wind. And then my thinking falls silent, waiting for His thoughts.

Minutes go by in total silence, except for the tick-tock of a wall clock. My mind focuses on the gentle cadence of the clock, and out of the rhythm comes a distinct stream of consciousness: "Serve Me with words…inspired by the Holy Spirit…His power…your spiritual story." The stream stops there. Does God want me to write a spiritual story of my life?

What is my spiritual story? Why would anyone be interested in it? "OK, Holy Spirit, what is your input?" I bow my head in silent expectation, buttressed by the many times He has answered that prayer. His still, small voice speaks into my interior mind, not audible in any sense of the word, but definitely not of my own making.

"In the last ten years, there has been more of God in your life most of the time. It was not always so. Start your story on the day I saved you."

✟ ✟ ✟

1982. Slowly and with much deliberation, I reach for my favorite pen, which lies in a groove in the desk designed for just such a purpose. A legal pad rests in the middle of the writing surface. With the guidance of the Holy Spirit, I begin the first paragraph of my spiritual story.

April 2, 1982 is the day He saved me. It didn't happen in a church or at a Billy Graham crusade or by someone handing me a Bible tract. It occurred in a hotel room on the western edge of Minneapolis, with no one else present. I was thirty-five then, rather old for a new convert, according to whoever keeps track of such things.

I was a reading and communication instructor at a college in Willmar, Minnesota and was in charge of a state-wide reading conference. I had never done anything of this magnitude before and was, quite frankly, frightened. In one hour I'd be standing in front of three hundred of my peers, many of whom I knew personally, giving the opening welcome and telling them what to expect for the next three days. There I'd be, a guy six feet tall and wearing a short beard but feeling like a naked ant wanting to crawl under the woodwork.

I sat in a straight-back wooden desk chair I'd put in the middle of my hotel room, for a reason I can't remember. I was in my dress suit, tie undone, struggling to mentally prepare for my opening introduction. The responsibility of the whole thing overwhelmed me. I found myself reciting the same first line over and over. It was the only thing I could keep in mind.

"Oh, Lord," I prayed, "Get me through this, and I'll follow you for the rest of my life. I can't do it on my own." I thought I was a Christian because I believed in my mind the gospel of Jesus' crucifixion and resurrection. But my belief had not transformed my will. Nor was it planted firmly in my heart.

I pleaded with profound passion: "Lord, help me! Lord, help me!" The arms of my suit coat rose toward the ceiling. Tears streamed from my eyes. "Lord, Jesus, have mercy on me."

From somewhere within me came a question: "Will you let Me live My life through you?" I did not hear it with my ears or see it in my mind, yet it was unmistakable. It was my first encounter with the supernatural.

I fell to my knees and cried out, "Jesus, I accept You as my Savior and Lord." It was not spoken out of my mind but somewhere much deeper. Trumpets did not blare and a light from heaven didn't come down, but I realized in an instant I was no longer the same person.

To accurately describe this coming to the Lord, I need to flip the calendar back a year. I first met Martin Swanson when the president of a printing company brought us together to work on a brochure. Martin was the artist and I the copywriter. His face was thin and his clothes hung from his body as if they were a size too large. I soon discovered he was a giant in his Christian faith, though he didn't pound on me with a Bible or make any demands. He was gentle in spirit and spoke with a voice I had to strain to hear.

I thought I was a Christian because I'd grown up in a Christian home, went to a Christian school for eight years, and was, at the time, an elder in a protestant church. But I was nowhere near measuring up to Martin in my faith. And I recognized it as we met often on the brochure.

As we worked together, Martin examined my faith in a quiet sort of way and found it lacking. I thought you had to earn your way into heaven, like racking up enough points on a credit card for a free plane ticket to Ireland. One day Martin told me, "Paul, no one can make it to heaven on their own. You have to accept Jesus Christ as your Savior."

He was the first one who told me there was a choice to make. I couldn't add Christ into my life like pouring cream into coffee. I needed to let Him take over my life, at my invitation. That's what Martin said, but I didn't get it.

After that first brochure, we collaborated on several other projects, which I fit in on a part-time basis after finishing my teaching job mid-afternoon most days. Martin was a freelance artist working out of his home. Sometime later, I think it was about six months, we were meeting for lunch to discuss a four-color brochure that would make both of us a good amount of money.

He asked in a nonchalant way how I was doing. I'm not sure what he was referring to, but I blurted out, "You know, Martin, I think I've finally come to understand what you've been telling me. If I could make it to heaven under my own power, then there'd have been no reason for Jesus to die on the cross. I realize I'm to abandon my natural life and hand it over to Him, but that's where I'm stuck. I don't know what abandoning my life means."

I was hoping Martin would enlighten me, but he didn't. "You've arrived at a good spot in your life, Paul. You know what you need. I'll pray you receive it." He changed the subject to a canoe he was building in his basement. He must have prayed with power because my salvation took place two days later, in the manner described at the start of this chapter.

I could hardly wait to return home and proclaim to Martin that the Lord had answered his prayers. We met for breakfast the next morning. I was giddy when we stood in the restaurant parking lot, which was a weird word to describe me. I was a man of the mind and not of the emotions. Yet, I dashed over to Martin and declared in a voice bordering on gushy, "I've been saved, Martin! I've been saved!" It was impossible to control my breathing as I told him all about the amazing encounter with God in my hotel room. "Everything is different now. I'm a new creation. I can't explain it with logic, but the clouds are whiter, the sky is bluer, and the air smells like spring. What I want for myself is no longer important. I'm filled with joy and want to follow Him and do what's important to Him." I was out of breath and could not say anything more.

Martin looked at me with bright eyes and a smile as warm as a sunbeam. He grabbed me with a "brothers-in-Christ" hug. The rest of the day was lost on me other than the episode in the parking lot.

I thought my joy would never end, but I was naïve. The day of salvation was a huge peak of bliss, but one comes back to earth after a time. My time was six months later.

2

Early Monday Morning, October 17, 2011. It was an impolite weekend. My wife, Molly, has been having a rough time with this. Her five-foot-two-inch frame sank below five feet as she shuffled around with her head down, her pretty face contorted with tears and frowns, her personality withdrawn. Her disposition alarms me.

She had not reacted this way with previous family crises. She was the solid one when our son Joe underwent an emergency appendectomy and when our other son Jack fell from the top of a ten-foot slide headfirst into the dirt below, suffering only a dislocated shoulder. I was the basket case with those two events. Now our roles have reversed. I'm the one dying of cancer but needing to be strong for her sake. She's the unnerved one.

She said to me at least ten times over the weekend, "Oh, Paul, I do not think I can go on without you."

My response was always the same, "You'll be able to, my dear. God will give you the strength." But what I said to myself was different: "If God can give her the strength, why doesn't He heal me instead?"

Molly and I visited our two sons over the weekend to deliver the bad news in person. The weather was cold for October, below freezing and with a bitter wind. Molly wore a heavy leather jacket, zipped up to the top, but it didn't keep her warm. I don't think a parka would have kept her warm.

We visited Jack's home in Northfield first, on Saturday. He was the apple that fell not far from the tree. We were alike in so many ways, other than outward appearance. He was a good two inches taller than I and had the body of a lumberjack. He knew something was amiss when he saw his mother, who looked as if she were on death row.

I gave him the bad news as we were standing in the living room; he fell back into a reclining chair with a thud. His face became pale and his breathing labored. It took almost a minute for him to compose himself enough to say, "No, I will not accept you're going to die in six months. It's a mistake. Catherine and I will pray that your next test shows no cancer." That's a prayer I'd been praying since Friday.

The rest of the visit was somber. We sat in the living room for hours, senselessly watching college football games. I don't remember now who played or any of the scores. I think Jack was more concerned with his mother than with me. He kept looking at her sitting on the couch with her leather jacket still zipped up and her eyes staring straight ahead. There was no talk of my condition at the dinner table. Our attention turned to our granddaughter, Margo, who had come home late afternoon from a birthday party and didn't know Grampa was deathly ill. Her parents were both good looking, but they couldn't hold a candle to her. She'd started middle-school in September and was chock full of information about her classes, friends, and new soccer team.

No one slept much that evening except Margo. Jack and Catherine chose to break the news to her after we left. Margo and I had a special bond since the time she was four when I started telling her made-up stories to develop her imagination. She'd say to me, "Grampa, tell me the wildest, craziest, most incredible story ever," and looked at me with anticipation. I would tell her tales about talking bears and princesses who overcame great hardships and genies who would grant any wish.

We left Northfield after church the next morning and drove to Joe's home in Minneapolis. Joe was different than Jack in many ways. He was two inches shorter than Jack but with a body sculpted out of steel, honed by years of weightlifting and playing football from fourth grade through college. He was also much more stoic than Jack. As we sat around the kitchen table, he suspected we were about to deliver bad news. He looked at his somber mother and must have thought it was about her.

"What's wrong, Mom? You don't look well." Joe was a man of few words who always got right to the point. He was chatty growing up but became more precise with words in high school and college. We attributed it to all the sports he played. The language that coaches and players use is purposely crisp because time is of the essence.

"It is not me who is ill, Joe. It is Dad." Molly could say no more as she sat at the table, head down, still wearing the leather jacket that could bring no warmth. She nodded toward me, so I told him I'd been diagnosed with terminal pancreatic cancer. His demeanor didn't change. He was a guy who saw life as a football game – you win some and you lose some.

I'd rarely seen him become emotional, but after several seconds of silence, he got up from his chair and stood by me, as a signal that I was to get up as well. Then he broke down and held me in his arms and wept. "Dad, this can't be happening. God won't let it happen." That's another prayer I'd been praying since Friday.

The rest of the visit was as somber as the Northfield one. Molly was not in a mental state to say much. I was not in a place where I wanted to go beyond telling Joe the essentials of how this had happened. Joe and I mindlessly watched NFL football games, snacking on chips and dip and nibbling on sandwiches as we watched the Vikings play the Bears. Molly sat in her coat and acted as if she were someplace else. Our team was down 26-3 at halftime, so Molly and I headed back home. The Vikings ended up losing 39-10.

I called my brother Teddy in Raleigh, North Carolina between games Sunday afternoon. He and I had a triple bond – brothers in blood, brothers in Christ, and best friends. When I finished the proclamation, I thought the call had been disconnected. "Are you there, Teddy?"

"I'm here." Teddy had a doctor's degree in psychology and was the spiritual guru of the Chambers family. He usually was not at a loss for words. "How are you doing, Paul?"

"How do you think I'm doing?"

"Probably not very well right now."

"I'm not, but that isn't what I want to talk to you about. Consider I'm one of your patients. How do I go on from here? What is my purpose for the months I have yet to live?"

Teddy was slow to answer, as if he had to ponder each word to construct a coherent sentence. "Let me…bring this to the Lord in prayer…so I'm not guiding you…out of my own…resources." As he prayed, I prayed also for the Holy Spirit to give Teddy the wisdom to speak and me the humility to listen. Teddy was two years older, and I'd always looked up to him for advice. I'd also looked up to him because he was four inches taller, sometimes more than that as we were growing up.

Several minutes passed before Teddy's voice came over the phone again. "Here's a thought for you to consider, brother. I've seen a remarkable change in you since the day you were saved. Your spiritual journey has been an inspiration to me and would be an inspiration to others. You could be an encouragement to Christians by how the Holy Spirit has directed your life. Why don't you think about writing a story telling how you came to experience more of God more of the time. It would give you the purpose you are looking for."

God never ceases to surprise me. Teddy confirmed the word I'd received from the Holy Spirit last Friday without my saying anything about it. "Teddy, let me tell you what the Holy Spirit suggested the day my doctor told me I had pancreatic cancer." I related the whole story. "Isn't God amazing?" I said as I concluded.

"Indeed He is," said Teddy from twelve hundred miles away. "Indeed He is."

It's Monday morning, and the sun is shining brightly in the eastern sky. One week from today I start my first chemotherapy treatment and am fearful. The doctor said it was not without side effects that vary with every patient. Some do well; some do horribly. I pray I'm one of the doing-well ones.

My pen is in the groove where I last left it and the yellow legal pad is waiting for the second chapter.

1982. Shortly after I was born again of the Spirit, Martin and I formed an advertising agency and became partners in a fledgling business venture. What a blessing it was to have the one who led me to Christ disciple me on a daily basis. But the business didn't grow as expected, and the wolf was at our doors, more so Martin's than mine. My wife had a teaching job; his was a stay-at-home mom. The worry of the business failing consumed me. Going after new clients was on the altar of my life; my passion for Christ was somewhere in a back pew.

A few months after we started our agency, Martin and I were discussing a new project over lunch in my office at work. His area was too messy. With all the busyness of our business, my spiritual life was as stale as the sandwich I was eating.

It was my turn to bless the food. I sputtered out a "God bless this food," and took a bite out of my sandwich. Martin had a concerned look on his face. "What's wrong, Paul? You haven't been an on-fire Christian lately."

"Is it that obvious?" I answered. He didn't reply, so I bluntly answered the question. "I've come down from the mountaintop, Martin, into a dusty valley; and I'm choking on the sand. I believe the flame of the Holy Spirit is as bright as it's ever been in my spirit; you've taught me that. But I can't see it any longer. What's happening to me? What can I do about it?"

"Two good questions, Paul." The smile was back on his face. "Let me tackle the first one. It was bound to happen."

"Bound to happen? Why didn't you warn me?" I was mildly upset. I wanted questions answered before I asked them. Martin believed questions were best answered in the context of one's experience.

"Because you would not have understood the warning. You were flying high on emotions. I'd never heard so many 'Praise the Lord' exclamations from one person before." At that point Martin started laughing. "You were on fire for the Lord. Who was I to quench it?"

"Well, something has quenched it."

"The same thing happens to most new converts. It's hard to sustain the passion of salvation without a foundation of knowledge."

"Knowledge of what?"

"Understanding how God interacts with us."

I replied, "The Bible is all about God's interaction with His people. I've been studying it daily, both the Old and New Testament."

"But you don't know what you're looking for." I didn't take that as an insult. Martin knew Scripture better than most believers.

I said matter-of-factly, "I expect you know what I should be looking for, or you wouldn't have brought it up."

"It's all right to be confused, Paul. God doesn't expect us to know everything right away. I was as unknowing as you half a year into my salvation. The man who led me to Christ told me to read *The Spiritual Man* by Watchman Nee. I think that book will help you as well. I'll bring my copy to work tomorrow. When you realize how incredible the interactions between God and His children are, you'll have your passion back."

3

Mid-Monday Morning, October 17, 2011. I tried to eat breakfast after the last chapter, but the dread of my condition took away my appetite. If I don't focus on something else and soon, I'll be frozen in fear. I hurry down the hallway to write the third chapter.

✞ ✞ ✞

1982. The next morning Martin handed me *The Spiritual Man* by Watchman Nee in a frayed paperback.

He had highlighted many passages with what was now a dim yellow. That evening after supper, I walked down the stairs into the lower level of our home and lit the kindling in the fireplace. Soon there was a yellow glow bathing the family room.

I sat down in my comfortable reading chair and started to read. The chair was well aware of all the books I'd pored over in it – hundreds of them – and wrapped me in a warm embrace. The title of the first chapter was *The Spirit, the Soul, and the Body.* I spent the better part of an hour reading and rereading pages seven through ten. In them, Nee compared spirit, soul, and body to a light bulb. "Within a bulb, there is the electricity, the filament, and the light. The body is like the filament, the spirit is like the electricity, and the soul is like the light." Nee continued with this explanation: "The body is the 'world-consciousness,' the soul is the 'self-consciousness,' and the spirit is the 'God-consciousness.'" Up to this time, I thought soul and spirit meant the same thing. Nee's explanation gave me knowledge I did not have, exactly what Martin said I needed. I absorbed the assumptions in the book like dry land taking in rain. The soul is our mind, will, and emotions. It is our personality, our temperament, and what makes each one of us uniquely us. Our spirit is where God lives. It made sense to me once it was presented with logic and an illustration.

An amber glow and warmth came from the fireplace and gave me a sense of well-being. "Hmm," I thought, "this explains my salvation. I was born with a spirit and a soul, but my spirit was lifeless until the Holy Spirit filled it at the moment of my salvation. Now He is the power-house that brings electricity to my soul." I had struggled with Nee's explanation of body, soul, and spirit up to the light bulb metaphor. Then it came alive.

I was excited and jumped out of my chair to fetch another log. I looked out the window on the south wall before sitting down and saw a bright full moon staring back at me from the west. As I was standing there, a thought came into my mind: "If the Holy Spirit is charging my soul, I should be a radiant light all the time. But I'm not. I'll ask Martin about that tomorrow morning."

I went upstairs to put the boys to bed and spend time with Molly, the love of my life and an even better friend than Teddy, if that were possible. "You seem happier tonight than you have been for the last few months. What happened?" Molly had been a Christian before me, so she understood my explanation of what I'd just read.

"Do you remember how afire I was for Christ last April when I accepted Jesus as my Savior and Lord?"

"I do. I had never heard so many 'Praise the Lord' exclamations in my life."

"And have you noticed that 'Praise the Lord' has slipped from my vocabulary of late?"

"I have, but chose not to speak to you about it. I felt it was something you needed to work out with the Lord and I did not want to get in the way. The last thing you need is a pushy wife." We both laughed.

"Well, that something I needed to work out happened tonight." I told her what I'd come to understand from reading Watchman Nee but didn't mention the missing piece.

Molly came over to the couch and sat down beside me. We held hands and talked about the amazing grace God gives to those who become part of His family.

Martin was at his easel when I arrived the next morning. His workplace looked like a wind had blown through and scattered client portfolios and sheets of drawing paper into little heaps. How he knew what was where, I could never figure out. Oftentimes, he didn't know either. The first order of business was always the same: we prayed for God's blessing on the day. After that, I posed my question from the previous night.

Martin's face had a smile on it, as it usually did. I wonder if God painted it on him with indelible ink. "That's a good question, Paul, and one Nee does not answer in the pages you read. You see, the Holy Spirit doesn't force Himself on anyone, even those whose spirits He fills. It's up to you, my friend, to open up your soul to Him, like turning on a light switch. That's how you become a bright light for Christ." Martin contemplated the illustration he was working on of a Minnesota Gopher football great.

I also looked at the illustration, admiring how talented he was. "I was a bright light all the time up to a few months ago, but I'm more often a dim glimmer these days. How do you explain that?"

Martin looked directly at me. His eyes were steely blue and penetrating. "It's not an on-off switch, you know. It's a dimmer switch that controls how much electricity we allow in."

"Ah! That explains it. My hand turning the dial determines how much Holy Spirit power I allow into my life."

"You've got it, Paul," said Martin, with the look of a professor who'd just imparted a gem of wisdom to his favorite pupil.

He continued looking through me, as if he could read my mind. "Now tell me, what does your hand on the switch represent?"

My mind went blank. "I don't know."

"Why your will, of course," answered Martin. "You decide how much of the power of the Holy Spirit you let into your life."

"Isn't life another word for soul?"

"That's correct. You understand Watchman Nee well."

His eyes went back to the illustration as I cleared a couple client portfolios off a chair and sat down to discuss the day's projects.

Martin made a quick brush stroke to the football player's face. "But will you remember what you read last night and what we discussed this morning?"

"What do you mean?"

"I mean you need to record the spiritual insights of your life soon after they occur, or you'll lose them. As a Chinese philosopher once said, 'The palest ink is better than the most retentive memory.'"

I gave him a quizzical look.

4

Monday Afternoon, October 17, 2011. Anxiety and worry have thrown Molly off the tracks. She dressed carelessly this morning in blue capris pants and a green sweatshirt that has seen better days. Her hair is uncombed. She pops into my office every few minutes to check if I'm still alive. How I wish I could put my hand on her arm and tell her it will be OK. But it won't be. The worst is yet to come.

An hour ago, as I was finishing the last chapter, she finally spoke. "Oh, Paul, what will I do without you?" She went to her knees and put her head on my lap.

"God will give you the strength to deal with this. Trust in Him." I used my preacher's voice. The truth is, I'm afraid and feeling hopeless. I'm not at the point of trusting in Him myself. How can I expect her to do so?

"Yes, I will trust in Him," she said in a faraway voice, without emotion, like a little child reciting her catechism.

I picked her up and held her in my arms. "Yes, we will both trust Him. What else can we do? But it will take time."

"Yes, it will take time," she responded and then started sobbing uncontrollably.

The bell is tolling for me. I need to block out negative thinking to write one more chapter.

✞ ✞ ✞

1982. What did Martin mean in his office that day about recording spiritual insights? "I'd suggest you keep a spiritual journal," he said while shuffling through several project folders to find the one he wanted. I watched with interest.

"Maybe you put it in your L file," I ventured.

"What L file?"

"Your favorite one. The big one with L for 'Lost' written on the outside. Really, Martin, you need to clean up this mess. Some evening I'm going to come out here and straighten up your files. And if they fall into disarray again, you're going to meet Jesus a lot sooner than you anticipated."

Martin laughed sheepishly and brushed the hair from his forehead back into its proper place. That's about the only thing he tried to keep straight. Maybe the creative side of him was so dominant that order was impossible for him. I was the opposite, the super-organized one, the follower of the old adage: "A place for everything and everything in its place."

I threw my hands up. "OK, Martin, let's forget about unsnarling your clutter. It's probably hopeless anyhow. Tell me about keeping a spiritual diary."

Martin threw his head back and laughed so hard he started to choke. "I'm glad you finally realize it's hopeless. It will make working together much more pleasant." His laugh tapered off, and he switched to his regular face. "It's not a diary but a journal."

"What's the difference?" I asked.

"A diary is something you write in every day. You use a spiritual journal to record the highlights of your Christian walk – the great things God has done in your life. If you don't write them down, you'll forget them." I waited for more, but Martin was like Joe, a man of few words.

"So I expect I review the highlights every now and again as reminders of God's intervention in my life."

"Right."

A few days later I drove to Minneapolis to meet with a new client. Her office was in a strip mall, next to a huge Christian bookstore. She wanted us to complete a twelve-page brochure in full color, as well as place several ads in high-circulation trade magazines. I was upbeat as I walked out her door and into the bookstore.

A clerk led me to four long shelves of Christian journals. There were large ones and small, hardcover and soft, embossed with Bible verses or plain. There was no end to the variations. Half an hour later, I walked out with a 7 ¼ inch by 10 ¼ inch hardcover book of dark blue with the words *My Christian Journal* imprinted on the front cover.

I was a new Christian, and highlights came at the rate of two to four a month. On March 24, 1983, I recorded my first vision.

> While driving to Minneapolis yesterday, I envisioned a road of a much different nature running parallel to the highway I was on.
>
> In a flash, I was walking on the other road, a path of smooth gravel, winding through woods and open spaces, with Christ ahead of me. He turned and spoke almost in a whisper, "Paul, come follow Me."
>
> I said, "Yes, Lord."
>
> He continued the conversation, "Do you see any need to pile up money for retirement?"
>
> I replied, "No, Lord."
>
> "Do you see any need for a new house, fashionable clothes, or a shiny new car?"
>
> "No, my Lord."
>
> "Are there any needs you have on this road?"
>
> "None," I answered. "To be with You is all I want. You will provide everything I need." With this confession, I experienced a feeling of great peace.
>
> Alongside the road were wild animals and monsters, but I knew they couldn't harm me because I was with the King. As we were about to enter a dense woods, I had a strong urge to turn around and go back a few hundred yards.
>
> "Lord, I wish to see for just a minute what I have left behind." I returned to an opening in the woods and noticed the path I was on with Jesus stood above a deep ditch with steep sides. The ditch was filled with various distorted figures personifying greed, envy, gossip, pleasure, dishonesty, immorality, alcoholism, and the other things of this world not part of the King's neighborhood. I also saw some real people, though I couldn't recognize anyone in particular.
>
> "Come down with us," the misshapen figures and people shouted. "Life is good here. Don't be a Goody Two-Shoes. A life of pleasure is the best life of all. This is where you'll find

happiness." But they didn't look happy, and a miry sludge lapped at their heels. I realized their lot in life was to slide back into that sludge, the whole dirty, tattered, and earthy lot of them. Yet, the ditch and what was in it tempted me.

Jesus showed up at that point and sighed, "Paul, come follow Me." Those in the ditch couldn't see Him. I realized if I crawled down into the ditch, I also would not be able to see Him. Eventually, I would forget Him, and the miry sludge would be lapping at my heels.

"Come, follow Me," Jesus repeated.

"Yes, Lord, I will follow You."

Those in the ditch heard the exchange and yelled, "You fool!" but they had no attraction for me anymore.

I was on the high road with my Lord, and that's where I desired to be. Psalm 73:25 resonated in my mind: "Whom have I in heaven but You? And earth has nothing I desire besides You."

My next vision came two years later.

5

Tuesday, October 18, 2011. The temperature was above 40 this morning, heading to 55. I went out for an early morning walk and a time of reflection, but before I left, Molly said, "How will I go on when you are gone?"

"I'll be back in thirty minutes," I said.

"This is not funny, Paul. I cannot see my life without you in it."

It was to have been a congenial walk with Jesus but deteriorated into a morbid introspection of the complete failure of my body. I couldn't pull myself out of negative thinking during the thirty minutes I was outside, even with the pleasant weather.

When I entered our home, I took the first door to my right into the office that was my workplace and prayer closet. I fell to my knees in the middle of the floor. "Lord, take away this focus on me, me, me. A piece of Molly's soul is being torn out. Concentrate my attention on her loss more than mine."

I got up from my knees and went into the kitchen. I shouldn't have joked with her in the state she is in. I shouldn't be wisecracking in the state I am in. She turned from the stove, and I grabbed her and pulled her close to me. "We need to trust in the Lord, Molly."

"I know, Paul, but it is so hard, so very, very hard." No more was spoken as we intertwined as one. I realized, for the first time, she is sharing in the end of my life as if she were the one dying. I need to be strong for her to be strong. I need to trust in God for her to trust in God. But it's so very, very hard. I want desperately to be healed but have doubts it will happen. I have told people God always answers prayer. Now it's personal, and I'm not so sure.

I have a new identity since last Friday. My next-door neighbor described the new me in four words when we were outside yesterday afternoon. After I broke the bad news, he put his hands to his face and said, "You are pancreatic cancer. No, I mean you have pancreatic cancer," he quickly corrected himself. He was right the first time. That's my new identity: the pancreatic cancer guy. What an oppressive thought! I strangle my pen in a death grip and start writing about another vision from the Holy Spirit that was convicting and life changing.

✝ ✝ ✝

1985. Three years later my second vision arrived. Before I was saved, I boasted of my self-sufficiency. The president of our college once remarked to me, "Paul, I've never met a man as in control of his life as you are. Nothing seems to faze you." I took that as a noteworthy compliment. I was indeed the master of my fate and proud of it. What a half-wit I was before the Holy Spirit came into my life with the other half.

Before coming to the college in Willmar, Minnesota, I had been an advertising manager for a large manufacturer in Minneapolis, leaving that job to complete a Master's degree in English Literature at the University of Minnesota. I was in control and doing well. When I was offered the job in Willmar, it was nothing more than I had expected. There was no need for me to become a Christian. It was six years later when Martin, God's messenger, planted the seed in my heart that there was a choice to make. "You can't go on as you are," he told me on more than one occasion. You know the rest of the story. I surrendered and gave up control of my life. Or did I?

When I accepted Jesus, there was Another who asked me to let Him take over. Sometimes the answer was yes; sometimes the old Paul ran the show. When I became an administrator at the college, supervising 35 technical programs and 100 faculty and staff, the spirit of control bounded back into my life like a frolicking dog.

I didn't realize I had fallen back into a control mode and needed a lesson from God's classroom. I was driving to Minneapolis when the Holy Spirit showed up with a vision, on a day so unseasonably hot the highway shimmered. This is my journal entry:

> In my imagination, I saw a bright, spacious, airy room on
> the top floor of a house I was living in. It was not anything I

had seen before. In that room were a sprawling mahogany desk, dark oak floors, and Venetian blinds that let the sun filter in. "This must be my spiritual office," I thought because Jesus was always there. I saw myself entering the room in the morning for an hour of prayer, worship, and Scripture reading. In that way, it mirrored what I actually did. When I left the room, Jesus did not go with me. I heard Him say, "Let Me go with you," but I ignored Him.

One morning, He suggested we tour the rest of the house; I reluctantly agreed. He led me to a small, dark room in a gloomy part of the house. He asked me to open the door, and I saw the inside of the room as He did – dingy and stuffy, with old rusty machinery controlled by shafts, levers, and other regulating mechanisms. I lowered my head in shame when Jesus revealed this was the control room of my self-life, left over from the days before I became a Christian. It was a place familiar to me and comforting, a room in which I spent way too much time.

Jesus looked at me with great sadness; it seemed as if He was about to cry. Without a word, His hand reached out for the key to this room. I hesitated. His hand stayed where it was, with palm upturned. How could I abandon the control room I grew up with? Jesus finally spoke in a gentle voice: "Give Me the key to your life." My hand shook as I handed Him the key. In that instant, I was transported to the edge of a vast ocean, listening to waves lapping on the shore, feeling a soft wind in my face, and sensing absolute freedom.

After what seemed to be an hour, I returned to the control room and stood there with Jesus. He looked deep into my eyes and said with authority, "Let Me destroy this room!" The experience of the ocean had changed my mind about what was best for me. Without hesitation, I answered Him with a nod of my head.

The control room disappeared in a powerful blast, and I found myself back in the spiritual office. It was ten times larger and brighter and fresher than the previous one, and was the only room in the house.

Seven months later, a raging blizzard replaced the shimmering highway and became an illustration of the condition of my soul. The warmth I felt in the spacious spiritual office was replaced by a coldness in my soul that arrived unannounced and unexplained. The Holy Spirit didn't send a vision to point out why I was experiencing a frosty interior life. He sent Joyce instead.

6

Early Morning, Wednesday, October 19, 2011. I was jolted out of bed at four a.m. by a dream in which a misshapen man was pushing me over the edge of a cliff. I woke up just before I tumbled down three-hundred feet into a bed of rocks. Now I'm at my roll-top desk in my pajamas, with a shaking pen and a need to take my mind quickly someplace else.

✝ ✝ ✝

1987. Farmers have good memories for the year something happened because they link it with weather extremes. The youngest daughter was born the year of a record drought. The favorite aunt died of cancer two weeks after a tornado knocked down the barn. Perfect weather resulting in a record yield of 80 bushels of wheat per acre was the year the farm debt was paid off.

The winter of 1986/87 was one of those weather extremes, unusually cold and snow piled up to the windows. This one, referring to both the weather and the condition of my soul, was the winter of my discontent, to borrow a line from Shakespeare.

No crisis of faith precipitated my spiritual apathy. No friend betrayed me. Things were fine with my family, job, and church. Yet, for some unknown reason, I was experiencing little of God most of the time. He was in the basement of my heart, and I rarely ventured down there.

Reading the Bible was a hapless chore. I prayed with no expectations because I was on an iceberg by myself, with God nowhere in sight. Even attending church held no joy. I needed to talk with Martin, but he had his own problems. His church was falling apart.

And a deranged patient was suing Teddy. Who else could I talk to? I felt alone.

The week following New Year's, I was the acting president of the college. Whoopty do! It only brought me grief, especially that Friday. I awoke early and put on a fashionable suit, navy dress pants, a formal shirt and tie, and classic wingtips. I needed to look the part. Why couldn't I be in Arizona vacationing in shorts and the real president back here in her tailored blazer?

I looked out our front window and saw nothing but snow. I called the college's weather forecaster – a custodian who lived thirty miles to the west. "It looks pretty bad out here, Paul. You'd better think about canceling school." I thanked him for the report and hung up the phone.

"Arghh!" I said out loud to no one in particular. Molly and the boys were not up yet. "If I cancel classes, the weather will improve within an hour. If I don't cancel, the snow and wind will turn into a raging blizzard."

I picked up the phone and called our local radio station. They predicted this would be the worst storm of the last three years and all schools in the area were shutting down. I sighed, "Could you please put out an announcement that we're canceling all classes, and send it to all the other radio and TV stations in your weather network."

According to our state college system, canceling classes and shutting down the college were two different things. If college employees wanted to be paid for the day, they had to show up or use a sick day. Most didn't want to use a sick day, so they showed up.

Molly and the boys were now up and had heard the news. Joe and Jack were overjoyed; they didn't have to go to school. Molly taught at our college and decided to take a personal leave day and stay home with our kids. The college president had to approve all personal leave days. The look on Molly's face told me it would be wise to approve her request. I pulled out of the garage and started driving to the college, usually a fifteen-minute trip.

The visibility from the front windshield was less than twenty feet, and snow drifted across the roads. I arrived at the college thirty minutes later, checked the radar, and saw nothing but heavy snow for miles and miles west. It would be a classic all-day-and-all-night squall. That made my next decision easy to make, which was to shut down the college. The notice I sent out brought great rejoicing. In less than five minutes, everyone flew out the doors, except for me and another administrator named Joyce.

She was a Christian who wore her religion on her sleeve, as the president of the college once said. I respected her for her bold stance; I was a more reserved believer. "Hmm," I thought. "I need Christian advice and Joyce is the only one was left. Are you behind this, Lord?" In my mind's eye, I saw a nod.

I entered her office and plopped down into a government-issued office chair that many a student had talked to her from. She was dressed in jeans and a sweatshirt, and a ratty parka hung by a hook on the back of her door. She was not a fashion plate even when classes were in session, but what she had on that day fell below her normal standards. Joyce was a few inches taller than Molly, and a bit plump. Her face was neither pretty nor ugly, a plain Jane so to speak.

She smiled and raised her eyebrows as if to say, "What's this all about?"

"Let me give it to you straight. I'm spiritually cold, Joyce. I've somehow lost the warmth of Jesus and don't know how to get it back." She waited for me to say more, but there was no more to say.

After a short time of silence, she replied with a casual "Well, well," and closed her eyes in prayer. Neither of us spoke for a minute. That was not unusual for her but made me uncomfortable. Slowly she lifted her head and put on a bemused smile. "Have you ever asked God how He sees you?"

I sat looking out the window. "That's an obvious question, Joyce, but I've never asked it of Him."

"Then perhaps you should."

"How do I do that?" I asked.

She stood up and said, "You'll figure it out, I'm sure," and grabbed her parka. "It's time to leave for anyone in their right mind. You'd better get out of here while you still can."

I stayed for an hour more wrapping up loose ends, not a very good decision with the weather delivering a knock-out punch. But I was a compulsive worker in those days, some said a workaholic, especially my wife. The phone rang, and it was her.

"I cannot believe you are still there, Paul. I thought you were stuck in a ditch on your way home. You had best leave right now. We are not able to even see across the street." Her declaration was more like a command than a request.

I put on my wool car coat and forced open the front door against a mound of snow. The snow in the parking lot was a foot high in some places. It would take a four-wheel-drive vehicle to get out, which is what I had. Snow boots would have been nice, but mine were in the side entry of our house. I prayed for God's hand to lead me home but wasn't certain He was up to the task. That's how far I had drifted.

I couldn't see much beyond the front of my truck. The road going past our college was narrow but fortunately very straight. It was a challenge to remain out of the ditch, whatever side I was on. Thank God, no one else was foolish enough to be out there.

I reached the main highway after a mile of white-knuckle driving. It was better than the road I had just left because the county snowplows had plowed it at least once. Piles of snow filled the ditches and blew across the highway, forming drifts as high as a foot that I thudded through with the gas pedal to the floor. It was like being in a different world where time stood still. Thud after thud after thud. God must have been pushing the back of my truck; otherwise, I couldn't have made it home.

The fifteen-minute trip took an hour. My body was spent and my mind exhausted as I pulled into the driveway and became hopelessly stuck half way to the garage, like a beached whale. I shoveled in front of the truck and behind, to no avail. It was time to take shelter someplace warm and safe.

7

Later Wednesday Morning, October 19, 2011. On the one hand, I'm exhausted from a short night of sleep. On the other hand, I need to keep writing or be haunted by that dreadful dream.

✝ ✝ ✝

The snowstorm of 1987 continued. I stumbled through the side door with snow crusted on my beard and eyebrows. My shoes were ruined, my coat had turned from black to white, and my pants were stiff and blotched. It must have been a pitiful sight.

"Joe and Jack wanted to go outside and help shovel," Molly said, "but I did not want to lose all three of you in one day."

"Good choice, my dear. It was brutal out there." I also thought they were too young to be of much help. They ran to hug me when my coat came off. Molly waited until I took a shower and put on dry clothes. My shirt was saturated with sweat, which bled into my sport coat. My pants were starting to drip in seventy-degree weather.

The three of them waited in the kitchen until I returned in jeans and a sweatshirt. Molly hugged me and said, "I was worried about you. I was afraid you would not make it home, stranded in some ditch somewhere." She gave me a kiss and wiggled her nose from the prickliness of my mustache, as she always did. "I am glad to see you alive."

"I'm glad to be alive. Would you mind terribly if I went downstairs by myself for a time? There's a conversation I'd like to have with God."

She probably thought I wanted to thank God for bringing me safely home, but what I really wanted was to ask God Joyce's question.

This wasn't the first time I'd gone downstairs alone to be with the Lord. I did it every morning.

"I know you did not have your morning time with the Lord because of the storm. The boys and I will stay topside until you invite us down. I will be praying for you."

"We'll be praying for you too, Dad," said both boys with one voice.

Molly handed me a hot mug of coffee as I headed downstairs. I put kindling under the partly burned logs in the fireplace and soon witnessed a roaring fire, with flames leaping up the chimney and a toasty yellow glow bathing the family room. I settled into my favorite chair, took a sip of coffee, and asked the question Joyce had suggested.

"How do You see me, Lord?" I hadn't expected an answer and was not disappointed.

I tried again: "Lord, You know all things, and I know so little. Please tell me how You see me." My mind remained deserted. I slumped in my chair and muttered, "Why bother with this? All I hear is my own thinking." A thought popped up from somewhere deep within me, "Be still and know that I am God." I heard only the ticking of a grandfather clock and lost track of my own thoughts. Out of the ticking came a whisper from the Holy Spirit, not audible in any sense of the word, but unmistakably not a product of my own thinking.

> By the seashore walks a man
> whose mind is like the ocean.

"What does that mean?" I spoke into my soul but heard only the steady ticking of the clock. After thirty minutes, I invited Molly and the boys down to watch the weather on TV. It monopolized the airways. I went to bed early and slept the sleep of the dead.

Saturday morning the storm had completed its wrath, and a roar came from near the side of the house. Our next door neighbor was blowing out our driveway after he finished his own. Ken was a man who loved his machine.

I meditated on the strange message during the first hour. It remained a puzzle. I grappled with it several times throughout the day and before going to sleep that night. This pattern went on for two weeks, but the riddle was still a riddle.

Though the Lord didn't explain the message, there was no doubt in my mind that He had given it to me and would reveal it by and by. In the meantime, a spiritual warmth melted the coldness of my soul. He loved me and spoke to me. And I loved Him anew. I felt as if I were born again, again.

The last two weeks of February brought down a wrath of Canadian air and historic blizzards. Then came March and spring break at the college where Molly and I worked. We deposited our two boys with Molly's parents in North Dakota for a week and took off for Beaufort, South Carolina, a legendary honeymoon destination on the Atlantic seaboard.

On the last morning of our vacation, I stepped out the back door of our rental home and walked fifty yards to the shore of the ocean, my venue for morning prayer time. I walked half a mile on the beach, sniffing the unmistakable smell of the ocean and feeling a friendly breeze brush my face. The vastness of the ocean made me understand my own smallness, and the Holy Spirit parlayed that thought into the meaning of "By the seashore walks a man…." I sprinted back on the hard-packed sand and wrote His revelation into my journal.

> I, the Holy Spirit, desire to fill your soul with the depths of God. Give Me your mind to think with, your will to decide, and your emotions to react. Stop looking to yourself for fulfillment and turn to God with all your heart and all your soul and all your strength. Let your mind become like the ocean. Then you will be a joyful Christian.

I looked up from my journal and shed tears. There was more to the Christian life than being saved. There was an ongoing communication with the Lord, and it was not one-sided. I had been good at praying but not listening. That changed after asking God how He saw me. And so I stayed close to the Lord and experienced more of Him most of the time, right? Wrong! The underlying cause of my spiritual deficiency had not yet been addressed. A year later, I was back to where I had been before talking with Joyce. My frustration knew no bounds. Why was I such a wavering Christian? Why did coldness inevitably follow spiritual warmth?

Not until a golf outing in Ellendale, North Dakota was the cause of my disquiet revealed and healed.

8

Thursday, October 20, 2011. I am trying to write the first sentence of the next chapter, but it is futile. The faces of my two sons haunt me. In a window of my mind, I see them standing in front of our car as we pull out from their driveways. Jack scrunches his shoulders as he stands motionless. His face lacks color. He tries to put on a smile as he waves goodbye, but it's pathetic. Joe paces back and forth like he's on the sidelines of a football game. The tears are gone, but his eyes are red and his face somber. It's the kind of look you see on a family member walking down the aisle after a funeral. He tries to wave but can't get his hand higher than his chest.

My older brother Tom mastered the art of blocking out troubles so he could focus on staying out of a nursing home. His workplace was either a wheelchair or a waterbed set up like an office. Both had portable desks that went around him. When he was in bed, he had a digital telephone dial beside him that he could hit with his right hand – the only part of his body, other than his head, that he could move, and then only upward. It was amazing to see him lift his arm and let it drop by gravity onto a huge dial that had preset phone numbers. I was number three.

His was a bleak road. Two years after his accident, his wife left him to establish a life of her own. She was a nurse and had been his primary caregiver. He had to hire round-the-clock help to provide for his needs, at a cost of nearly $100,000 a year. All caretakers doubled as secretaries to assist him in his many business ventures.

Whatever health complications a quadriplegic could have, Tom had. Besides that, he had single-father problems and business challenges. For thirty-three years, there were daily little problems, weekly medium problems, and at least one major problem a month.

He sold life insurance policies from his bed and wheelchair. He had a van with a lift and floor attachment to make business visits. He also used it for all his kids' sporting events both in Fargo and throughout North Dakota and Minnesota. And he rarely missed a North Dakota State football or basketball game.

But the insurance business did not bring in enough money for all his expenses, even though he was a lifetime member of the Million Dollar Roundtable. He needed other sources of income. At one time or another, he sold long-distance telephone packages, pots and pans, health foods, air purifiers, and I don't remember what else. In the last ten years of his life, he wrote a book about hidden handicaps and became a business coach to sales companies and individuals. He also was a featured presenter at large sales conferences and produced webinars on overcoming the psychological barriers to success – things such as anger, fear, insecurity, and a lack of understanding proven sales techniques.

Five years before he died, I asked him, "Tom, how can you concentrate on everything you are doing, given all your health problems, money problems, caretaker challenges, and family issues? I have trouble writing an ad when an investment I've made goes bad."

He answered with a smile, "If I thought about my problems, I'd never be able to earn enough money to stay out of a nursing home. I've gotten pretty good at blocking out negative thoughts."

"But how? I understand the concept of blocking out negative thoughts, but I'm not able to put it in practice"

He smiled with his let-me-tell-you-about-life look. "I have taught myself not to think about problems until I *can do* something about them or *have to do* something about them. For example, if I knew the police were coming to arrest me tomorrow morning for bank fraud, I could go to a basketball game tonight and thoroughly enjoy it. I wouldn't think about going to jail until the doorbell rang at 8 a.m."

"How did you master that technique?"

He laughed like a joke smith. "It's simple. I've had lots of problems."

I looked out the window at a UPS truck delivering a package to our front door and thought, "How can I transfer Tom's strategy to my problems now?" Well, there isn't anything I can do about my cancer right now or anything I have to do, not until next Monday. But there is something I can do – continue writing my story. As I open the front door to see what the package is, I'm reminded how God attends to even the smallest of needs. I'm on my last legal pad and here are a dozen new ones I ordered last week.

✝ ✝ ✝

1988. Ellendale was Molly's hometown, and we were visiting her dad in a nursing home over a long weekend. I took two hours off to play nine holes at Ellendale Country Club on a Friday afternoon.

I still didn't know why I had turned spiritually cold the previous year or yet again this year. My emotions were like the changing seasons of the year – cold, warm, hot, cool, and cold again. I was like a man with bipolar disease, bouncing around between the extremes of manic and depressive. I was frustrated and angry. I needed more than a Holy Spirit correction every time I drifted away from God. I needed major surgery, and the Ellendale golf course was the operating table.

The wind was blowing with determination as I walked down the first fairway of the course, a solitary figure leaning forward to withstand gusts up to twenty-five miles per hour. My eyes watered from a strong blast, so I couldn't see the green to hit my second shot. I stood forlornly in the fairway, putting my head down to protect my face from the fierce wind. Then I lifted my eyes to heaven, raised my arms, and shouted, "Tell me what's wrong!" It was unusual no one else was playing golf at the time and fortunate because anyone else would have thought I was deranged.

My pitiful cry resulted in a visual response from the Holy Spirit.

Two pictures appeared in my imagination, each portraying a different world. I was at the forefront of the first canvas, with Jesus in the background. On the second canvas, Jesus was at the forefront, and I was standing behind Him.

In an instant I could see why I was spiritually up and down. I was living in the wrong world much of the time. Shot by shot, hole by hole, my mind wrestled with the significance of the two scenes. In the first picture, I saw two gray spirits hovering near me at the front of the canvas. One was the dark spirit of the natural world promising wealth, material possessions, friends, and pleasure. The second was the shadowy spirit of my own natural self, filled with pride, self-importance, self-reliance, self-righteousness, and a perverse disposition to serve God my own way.

Somewhere on the third hole, I thought of the day of my salvation when I promised to follow Jesus with all my heart and with all my soul. I did so for some time, but eventually the pledge slipped into the recesses of my mind and the dusty cellar of my heart. "Why!" I asked God loudly with defeat in my voice, "can I not keep a commitment to live in Your world every waking minute?" It was fortunate I was alone on the course, for the echo of that desperate cry reverberated across two acres.

On the fourth hole, in a more subdued voice, I prayed, "Lord, save me from this capricious heart." I was drawing near to God and He was drawing near to me. The Holy Spirit placed this thought into my mind: "Your God is a God of a thousand chances, who brings to mind that which has been misplaced or covered over."

Walking down the eighth fairway, I pondered the great dilemma of living a spiritual life: how to be in the world but not of it. I said aloud, as if the Holy Spirit were standing alongside me, "How can I have more of God in my life, amidst all the things of the natural world that demand my attention – a checkbook to balance, a golf swing that needs tweaking, car tires that should be replaced, a birthday card to get out on time, and all the other details of my life?"

With the last putt on the ninth hole, the Holy Spirit gave me a thought that concluded the matter, which I expressed with these words: "My self-life and the dark spirit of the world pressure my heart and my soul like powerful waves breaking over me. I must die to myself and the world in some way, but it is so difficult." It would have been more accurate to say it was impossible.

"Jesus help me," I pleaded while putting my clubs in the car. "Push the focus on myself out of my soul to make room for You. Let me never again drift so far from You that I can't feel Your presence. Help me live in Your world, not mine – all the time." I spoke that prayer with utmost sincerity but without the wherewithal to carry it out. I simply couldn't get it into my head I didn't have what it takes. I was too easily distracted. The granddaddy of all distractions came a year later at the college where I worked, and I wasn't prepared for it.

9

Friday, October 21, 2011. Haunting voices play in my mind and disturb my thinking. "Paul, I can't live without you," bemoans Molly. Jack pleads, "Dad, you can't leave us. This is a mistake." Joe puts on a courageous front: "You'll beat the odds, Dad. I know you will."

My own interior voice adds, "Lord, take this death sentence away from me. Please let me live." I paced throughout the house, upstairs and down. Molly broke her silence when she saw my distress.

"What is wrong?"

I told her about the voices. "I can't write a word."

"Darling, you told me yesterday how your brother Tom taught you to block out negative thoughts and you were able to write a chapter. There is nothing you can do right now to change your circumstances, not until next Monday when you start the chemo. I am praying it will arrest the cancer."

It surprised me how much she said. I didn't know she'd even heard me yesterday when I told her about blocking out. Her two-hour appointment with a Christian counselor late yesterday afternoon must have done wonders. I'm happy to have her back.

I thanked Molly for the reminder and thought to myself: "I do need to block out those voices, but they're so loud. Lord put in me the ability to do as Tom did."

I stepped outside to breathe in the crisp fall air and clear my mind. An elderly neighbor came by walking her dog. Emily is also dying of cancer and looked at me with compassion. "You're struggling with your disease, aren't you?"

"How can I not be? It doesn't seem fair," and I told her about one cancer following the other.

"It's not meant to be fair," she said. "Life has never been fair if you look at it from the world's viewpoint. I've chosen a different vantage point – not the world now but the world yet to be, where everything is fair." She smiled a glorious smile and went on her way, with her little dog wagging its tail behind her.

I remember when Emily was first diagnosed with cancer and how hopeless she felt. She looked like a little old lady walking to the cemetery when she went outside to pick up the mail. Molly became her confidant, and they drank gallons of coffee over her kitchen table. Her brother, pastor, and a couple of hometown friends added to her support network. She had been walking steadily south as a helpless victim, then gradually turned to the north and into the arms of her Savior. There was hope after all.

I went inside and put on my writing slippers, comfortable pants, and a sloppy shirt. I'm ready to write.

1989 was the year our state system of higher education forced our technical college to merge with the community college right alongside us. I was responsible for pulling together two institutions that didn't want to get married. The faculty unions of each college were openly hostile; the two non-teaching staffs felt threatened. The operative word for describing the other side was "they." To make matters worse, the educational platforms of the two colleges drew different sorts of students. Trying to reach the dissimilar prospects with a common marketing theme brought criticism of me from both sides. "You're favoring *them*."

During this season of bitterness and infighting, I put my relationship with God on the back burner, as I tried to keep the pots on the front burners from boiling over. It was like juggling tigers, one mistake and they'd eat me alive. I drove to work at the crack of dawn instead of spending an hour in prayer, worship, and reading Scripture. I was too busy during the day to pray or keep the Lord in mind. My assistant said to me, "Paul, if you keep up this pace of activity, you're going to keel over. If I could help more than I am, I would. But I don't want to collapse either."

God could have smoothed the way had I asked Him. But it was all me, me, me, and it, it, it. My hair was shaggy and my beard scruffy because I didn't have time for a cut and trim. Molly laid out my clothes each night so I didn't have to do it in the morning.

Exhaustion followed me home every night. I only had the energy to eat, watch an hour of TV, and go to bed early. My kids asked why I acted as if they were not there, and Molly was disheartened by the manner in which I was conducting myself. I felt guilty, but what could I do? There was a college to save.

I also ignored the Holy Spirit; and the farther I distanced myself from Him, the less I recognized it. I had once asked Him to let me know when I was drifting so far from God I couldn't feel His presence. He chose the venue of a softball field just west of Lake Calhoun in Minneapolis to teach me a lesson from God's classroom.

I'd started running during the summer of my twenty-second year when it wasn't yet fashionable to loop around a quarter-mile track four times without being in some sort of race. Running exhilarated me and became a lifetime habit, eventually evolving into a regular jog of three miles, five times a week. My favorite running setting of all time was the three-mile path around Lake Calhoun. It was a popular walking, running, and biking site at the time, and still is.

I was a gregarious fellow by nature and in the habit of starting up conversations with people I'd never met or even seen before. It might be, for example, a person standing behind me in a grocery checkout line, or a stranger running around Lake Calhoun at about my speed. I'd run up behind him and ask, "How are you doing?" And he'd answer that he was running to clear his head for a new job he'd be starting the next day. Two miles later, I knew about the work he did, the family he had, and the church he attended.

A large softball field, which doubled as a soccer and lacrosse area, sat on the west side of Lake Calhoun, and it's where I always ended up after a run, walking across the outfield and the infield to an aluminum bench on the first-base side. There I'd sit and rest up from the run.

August 6, 1989 was a torrid summer day, at the same time my spiritual life was in the refrigerator, placed there by me as I dealt with the turmoil of the college. For the previous four months, I rarely opened the refrigerator door. I don't think I even knew where it was most of the time. I'd strayed far enough from Jesus that I was in danger of not knowing how to find my way back. I was not lost from my salvation but my working it out was absent without leave.

I'd just finished a college meeting in St. Paul and thirty minutes later was changing into running clothes at my usual parking spot by the field, hoping no one would walk by and see what I was doing. I was especially nervous about taking my pants off and putting on running shorts. I was afraid a cop would drive by and arrest me for indecent exposure.

The weather was tropical, near one-hundred degrees; and the humidity was so steamy a lake fog shimmered over Calhoun, giving the water a surreal look. I was the only one on the running path. Many times I wanted to stop but plodded on. My running rules dictated that if I stopped to rest, the run wouldn't count. So I jogged on deliberately, step after weary step, the sweat on my face nearly blinding me. The only thing that kept me going was the thought of the bench at the end of the run. After running for what seemed like a week, and staggering across left field, I plopped down on it, exhausted in body, mind, emotions, and will. It was the perfect classroom for the Holy Spirit to convict me of being an anemic Christian.

He caught me by surprise that sweltering summer day as I slumped on the bench about to expire and placed in my imagination the following picture.

I am standing at the steering wheel of a large ship with hundreds of sailors watching me. I am the captain and stare straight ahead into a gray fog. A man surrounded by a bright light offers to steer the ship, but I say, "I am the master of my fate: I am the captain of my soul," a verse I remembered from the poem *Invictus*.

That's the thought that governed me before I became a Christian. Now I hated it, yet the Holy Spirit showed me it was driving me once more.

The scene of the ship awakened me to my foolishness. "No, Lord. It's not my way but Your way." I bowed my head and prayed, "You are the captain of my soul. You are the master of my fate. Right here, right now, I rededicate myself to a deeper relationship with You. I will let You live Your life through me no matter how busy I am."

The Holy Spirit did not sing hallelujahs or lift me supernaturally off the bench, but I sensed deep within me that He was back in business in my life. I would no longer be a loner trying to solve the college-merger chaos: He would be my guide. I decided then and there to listen to Him and put myself on the back burner.

I stood up without the heaviness I'd been carrying, walked across the field, and drove home. Molly was in the kitchen when I walked up the side-door steps. She came over to give me a perfunctory kiss hello, but I knelt down before her. "I'm sorry for the way I've treated you and the boys. I've been so full of myself and so full of all I had to do. I pushed the three of you to the side. I pushed God aside as well. What a fool I've been! What an unmitigated fool!" I don't remember what else I said, but it must have made an impact on Molly.

She lifted me to my feet and gave me a crushing hug. I didn't think she was that strong. She grasped my head and kissed my face repeatedly, like I'd just come home from four years of combat. "Oh, I have prayed so hard that you would come to your senses, darling, and now you have. How did it happen?"

I related the Lake Calhoun story and started to cry. "God is so good."

"He is so good," she repeated. "Welcome home."

I ran to the living room and grabbed my two boys and spent the rest of the evening wrestling with them and telling stories of when I was a young boy their age. They loved those stories because I was such a rascal and always getting in trouble. I thank God they were not at all like me in that respect. They thought it funny that an old fuddy-duddy like their father could have been such a mischief-maker.

10

Saturday, October 22, 2011. I have my highlights journal open to the year 1991 and found an entry that moves me as deeply now as it did then.

The Lake Calhoun rededication began a transition in my spiritual status from more of God some of the time to more of God more of the time. A sermon in Fargo, North Dakota that would take place next year completed the transformation.

1991. I began asking questions of the Holy Spirit on a regular basis, such as "How do I handle this?" or "How do You want me to serve You here, Lord?"

One day I asked what my responsibility was in raising my two sons – Joseph who was fifteen and Jack who was eleven. The Holy Spirit gave me this thought: I should be more involved in their spiritual development instead of depending solely on our church.

Joe was starting to look like the football star he would become – still lanky and lean but starting to add bulk and muscle. He had reached the age where he saw his own potential and started lifting weights and doing other exercises to become an all-conference running back and all-area strong safety the year he graduated from high school. One winter, when Joe was ten, a preacher came to our church to give a series of messages on Revelation. At the end of each presentation, he asked people to come forward if they wanted to receive Christ. At the second session, Joe wanted to go up to the altar. I was not prepared for that and asked what he thought would happen up there. His answer led me to believe he was not yet ready to make a choice for Christ, so I held him back. I instructed him on what it

44

meant to be a Christian, and a year later he became saved at an evangelical crusade that rolled through Willmar.

Jack had a more sturdy build than Joe and would grow up to be two inches taller. He'd be a fullback by the time he reached his junior year, but right now he was more like a cuddly teddy bear. His bedtime ritual was to have me sit on his bed and tell him fanciful stories about a boy his own age named Tommy. One evening, when he was eight, I told him about the night Tommy accepted Jesus as his Savior, with all the accompanying joy and delight of becoming a real Christian. There was a pause of several seconds as little Jack contemplated the story. Then he said, "Dad, I want to become a Christian just like Tommy." That very night, through the power of the Holy Spirit, I led him to Christ.

I gathered them together one Wednesday evening for what came to be our weekly Bible study; it always took place in the lower level of our home, near the fireplace. "Tonight's lesson is on the two choices a rich young man had to make. It's told in three of the four gospels."

"That must mean it's an important story," suggested Jack.

"Good insight, Jack. That's true. Let's read the account in the 19th chapter of Matthew."

When we finished reading, I asked Joe, "What do you think?"

"I think the rich young man kinda had the same choice we all do. You know, follow Jesus or go your own way. I mean this guy thought he had it all together spiritually until Jesus told him that following the Ten Commandments wasn't good enough. No way."

"Absolutely right, Joe. Being good isn't good enough. Jesus gave him two choices, but the young man desired a third – to keep his riches and follow Jesus. He wanted to be rich in himself and rich in Christ as well. But that isn't an option. You either give up ownership of *all* you have, physical possessions as well as your mind, will, and emotions; or you don't. There's no in-between, no compromises, no hedging bets. It's all or nothing."

"But we're both saved, Dad," said Joe. "We made that choice. Why spend an evening on what's already happened?"

"Well, Joe, in a way it's a one-time choice, but in another way it isn't. To choose His path for our lives is one thing. To stay on that path year in and year out is a day-by-day choice, sometimes even a minute-by-minute one. In my own life I try to stay on the true path all the time, but every now and again, I wander off it for one reason or another."

Joe sometimes worked for my good friend Bennett MacDonald on his farm, sixty miles away, during the summer and had picked up some of his manners of expression. "How does that work out in real life, Dad?"

I smiled. "You've learned a lot from Ben, haven't you son? Do you remember how tough it was for me last year, trying to make a technical college and a community college into one college?"

Jack piped in. "We worried about you, Dad. Joe and Mom and me spent lots of time praying for you when you came home after dark."

"I appreciate that Jack. It's probably what brought me back to God's path instead of the ones I had been wandering on." I chose not to mention the run around Lake Calhoun, but then their prayers might have been the very thing that prompted the Holy Spirit's wake-up call.

"What paths were those? Dad," asked Joe.

"Well, there was a path called 'I can figure this out,' and another named 'Who can I contact to help me through this?' Finally, I came to a lonely road called 'It's hopeless and there's nothing I can do to make things better.' By that time, I was so far from God's path I didn't know what direction to go to find it again. All I could do was give up and let the Holy Spirit bring me back. I prayed a prayer of surrender and was returned to the main road. Once there, I stayed so close to Jesus that I could touch the hem of His cloak. I listened to Him instead of the clamoring voices of two embattled faculties. As I look back now, it *was* a hopeless situation – from a natural standpoint. But God is the God of hopeless situations, and He was my deliverer…once I totally depended on Him. It didn't all go perfectly. I wasn't praised as a hero, but it was manageable in the end."

The two boys looked at me with love and admiration in their eyes. "You're a hero to us, Dad," they said in unison. It was a teachable moment as I told them God was the hero in the story, not me.

11

Saturday Afternoon, October 22, 2011. Molly returned home from another counselor appointment. She's back to her full height again, with her back straight and her head uplifted. Her lovely face has lost its gloom, and she's wearing fashionable clothes.

"What happened with your counselor? You are as happy as a clam at high tide."

"Counselor-patient secrets," she said with a broad smile.

"C'mon now. I'm your husband."

"I will eventually tell you, my darling, but I need to process it first. I can say in general that I have come to grips with your condition and how I am to deal with it by becoming a supporting wife instead of a millstone around your neck."

"You're not a millstone around my neck."

"Oh, yes, I have been."

"No, no. You did the best you could." I was happy to see her cheery self again.

She walked over to the office chair I was sitting in and gave me a kiss on the cheek. Then she put her arm around my shoulders and whispered in my ear. "I think it is time for you to call it a day."

"I'd like to finish one more chapter, my dear, because next Monday's chemo will curtail my writing for probably a day or two. This is the chapter that kick-started me from more of God some of the time to more of God more of the time. It's a good place to rest for a few days."

"That must be the Fargo, North Dakota chapter," she replied. We had talked about that marvelous day many times since it happened. It was a landmark moment, like when the Israelites piled up rocks on the opposite shore after crossing through the Jordan River on their way to Jericho.

"All right. One more chapter, but that is it."
I agreed.

The sermon in Fargo happened on April 26, 1992; and, trite as it may sound, my life was never the same again. My knowledge of the Christian life had advanced over the past ten years. I read Scripture daily, belonged to a Bible study group, and learned much from Martin, Teddy, and several spiritual partners. I had experienced visions, revelations, and spiritual awakenings. Yet, something essential was missing, a secret the Holy Spirit gifted me in a church in North Dakota.

My white-haired and slightly hunched-over mother lived in a neat and orderly apartment in Moorhead, Minnesota at the time. She was eighty-four years old. I'd come a hundred and sixty-five miles to spend the weekend with her, out of a mixture of love and duty. My father had entrusted me to take care of Mom a year before he died, and this weekend was the seventh anniversary of his passing. Louise, for that was her given name, remembered Joe's passing with great sadness, for she had loved him deeply.

Big Ben in London is accurate to within one second of the most precise atomic clock. Mom was not far behind when it came to her Sunday morning routine. At 9:15, a faithful parishioner from St. Joseph's Church came to pick her up for the 9:30 service and brought her back home one hour and twenty minutes later. It was just in time for her to watch a live televised service from Messiah Lutheran Church in Fargo that started at 11:00. There was something about the quaint setting of Messiah and the humility of the pastor that appealed to her.

Visits to my mother's usually incorporated the whole family – Molly, Joe, Jack, and me – but this was a special weekend. On the times the whole family visited, we followed the first part of Mom's routine, attending the 9:30 service with her at St. Joseph's. The second part of her pattern – watching the Messiah service on TV – was replaced by satisfying the hunger of two growing boys. We headed straight to the Village Inn for breakfast after church.

My mother assumed she and I would follow the same breakfast routine this Sunday, but I had a surprise in mind for her, something to brighten her disposition. We first went to the St. Joseph's service, which was a somber one for Mom, for this was the day of Dad's passing.

Following the service, we walked out the double wooden doors into the bright sunshine and headed to breakfast, or so Mom thought. We drove right past the Village Inn and turned onto an on-ramp for Interstate 94, a half-mile away. "Where are we going, Paul?" she asked. "We passed the Village Inn."

"You'll see Mother; you'll see." She remained quiet the rest of the trip. She loved surprises and her mind was probably spinning with all the possibilities of where we might be going.

At one point, however, she couldn't restrain herself. "Oh, Paul, we're going to the Iron Skillet in Fargo where your father and I used to have breakfast." In fact, Dad had taken her there two days before he died of a heart attack in their living room. But we passed the off-ramp to that restaurant, and she shook her head in puzzlement.

When I turned into the parking lot of Messiah, she clapped her hands in delight. For her, this was a surprise to end all surprises. Even though Fargo was just across the Red River from Moorhead, Mom didn't have a car to make the trip and didn't want to impose on friends. A warm wind was gently blowing the leaves of the surrounding trees in a peaceful rhythm as we walked to the front door and into the lobby. We chose a pew near the front of the church so Mom could be near the action. The aroma of last Sunday's Easter lilies was still in the air. I watched her survey the inside of the church with meticulous care, from the back to the front, from the stained glass windows on the west to the Easter decorations still on the east wall. It was as if she were in an art gallery seeing all her favorite paintings up close for the first time. She was so busy taking in her surroundings that she didn't say a word to me. The radiant look on her face told me she was happy amidst the pain of this day.

The service began when a middle-aged man, a bit short and a bit pudgy, quietly stepped out from a side door, dressed in a simple white liturgical robe and gold stole. The buzz of conversation stopped the instant he stepped onto the altar area, and all eyes turned to him. He spoke in a soft voice and proceeded through the liturgy with great reverence. Hymns were sung and prayers were prayed, and then Pastor Lee stepped into the pulpit. The congregation was prepared to hear another inspirational sermon. The title was *The Unter Melody* (unter being the German word for under). I had been thinking about a golf game I'd played a couple days ago, but the Holy Spirit gave me a nudge I couldn't ignore: "This sermon is for you."

Pastor Lee looked out at his congregation with the love of Jesus on his face. His eyes pierced my soul, as if he were looking directly at me. His face glowed in an angelic way. He drew in a deep breath and revealed the underlying message of his sermon. "Underneath the song of this world, filled with family, friends, food, jobs, and everyday events, plays the subtle melody of the Holy Spirit; and if we desire with all our heart to stay near Jesus, that melody should fill our mind, will, and emotions every waking hour." Those forty-six words burned into my mind like a branding iron. I remember them exactly to this day.

The Holy Spirit used Pastor Lee's message to electrify my soul, and every word he preached added more power. As I left Messiah arm in arm with my mother, I was also arm in arm with the Holy Spirit. This sermon was only the first lesson in the course the Holy Spirit was teaching me; others on the same theme were soon to follow.

MORE OF GOD MORE OF THE TIME

1

Thursday, November 3, 2011. Ten days of my life are missing. Ten pounds of my flesh have disappeared into the atmosphere. The chemotherapy was a disaster. Nausea, vomiting, diarrhea, and mental fogginess spread over me like a heavy mist. I felt as if I'd been dropped into the bottom of hell. Dr. DeAngelo said mine was as bad a reaction as he'd seen. There will be no second treatment. I'm still wobbly this morning and unable to write more than this one paragraph. I pray to be better tomorrow.

Friday, November 4, 2011. After I threw up for the fifth time yesterday, I grumbled to Molly, "I believe writing my story is at an end. The chemo has disabled my body and my mind and my emotions. It has sucked the life out of me." My face was as white as the bedsheets. My hands trembled. My mind was unhinged.

"You are not giving much credit to God," she answered, in a voice that was firm but not stinging. "You have spoken to me so many times about letting go and letting God that it has become a mantra for me. It is time for you to put into practice what you have preached."

"That's pretty tough talk," I sputtered. "I feel like death is just down the street, and I'm heading that way."

Tears flowed down her cheeks and she said, "I am sorry. My counselor said I am supposed to give you a dose of tough love when you start feeling sorry for yourself. I should not have followed her advice until your health improved."

"No, that's OK. I need tough love. I'll be better tomorrow." I didn't think I would improve the next day but was willing to say anything to make Molly feel better. It worked.

It's now tomorrow and I *am* feeling better. The nightmare is over…for now.

I walked from the bedroom to the kitchen where Molly was boiling water for my morning oatmeal. I gave her a warm hug. No words needed to be spoken by either of us. The closeness of our bodies carried the message from yesterday that truth had been spoken and accepted. We held on to each other until the water boiled over onto the surface of the stove. Our laughter was the final release of tension.

I'm back in my office and ready to write. "Thank You, Lord, for Molly. Bless her, bless her, bless her."

The sun is in hiding, the temperature below freezing, and dark clouds are coming in from the west. I pray this isn't the first day of snow. I want to experience more fall weather. My goal is to complete one more chapter today, from the early 1990s.

✟ ✟ ✟

July 1992. The second lesson on the same theme arrived at a church in Northfield, Minnesota three months later.

Molly and I were there on a Saturday afternoon in July to welcome Jack and his family to their new home. The moving truck was already in the driveway. Jack had been transferred to Northfield, and it was a long trip up from Birmingham, Alabama, their previous home. This was a coming back to Minnesota for Jack but not for his wife. She was Alabama born and bred, in the magic city of Birmingham. Catherine was tall, slender, good-looking, and spoke with a Southern accent.

Saturday afternoon and evening were exhausting. The movers did the carrying in, but the two Chambers families did all the arranging. I was the only one able to get up the next morning for a Sunday service and headed out to a church I'd found on the internet. But had *I* really found it? Looking back now, I can see the Holy Spirit guiding my hands on the keyboard to find Life 21 Church, a small house of worship tucked away on a side street on the south side of town.

The weather was curiously singular that morning. The sky was overcast, a solid gray without any distinctive shapes, like a fog about to settle on the ground. The temperature was neither hot nor cold. I walked through the front doors of the church and into a hallway filled with faces I'd never seen. I was immediately approached by Gary, one of the elders of the church. We conversed in the usual get-acquainted kind of way when suddenly, without transition, Gary's eyes lit up and his voice took on the tone of a man revealing a special secret. "This is a church of high expectations, Paul, and the Holy Spirit will do great things this morning." I had no idea what he meant, and I don't think he knew exactly what he meant either. But the Holy Spirit knew.

The service started with praise and worship music. The worship team's final song was *Jesus, Lover of my soul; Jesus, I will never let You go*. It was gently reaching its conclusion when the lead guitarist, a young woman named Libby, began softly playing a different melody with different words. The new melody seemed to float underneath the main melody, so subtly I could barely hear it at first. The volume of this under melody gradually increased until I could hear the music and her words more clearly. It was captivating beyond description.

Gradually, the other musicians transitioned to the melody Libby was playing and the phrases she was singing, adding praise and worship words of their own. This under melody, which was now the only melody, continued for at least ten minutes. The congregation, including me, was greatly affected. Some stood in the aisles with heads bowed, many fell to their knees, and a few came forward and lay prostrate before the altar. I sat with head in hands, overwhelmed by it all.

After the service, I approached Libby and asked if the worship team practiced the last song the way it unfolded. She smiled and said, "No." A nudge from within prompted a follow-up question: "Was it the Holy Spirit who directed you to play the new song?" She smiled again and said, "Yes."

Upon leaving the church, I sat in my car for several minutes in awe with what I'd just experienced. Pastor Lee's under melody sermon three months earlier had just been linked to an under melody hymn at a church in Northfield. I knew the Holy Spirit had connected the two happenings but was at a loss of how to explain it with a rationale mind. It seems in my spiritual life that the Holy Spirit works with sequences of three. I expected another link to appear in due time and was not disappointed.

2

Saturday, November 5, 2011. A panic attack took hold of me and shook me yesterday morning five minutes after typing the last sentence of the previous chapter. It was the most horrible thing I'd ever experienced; I thought I was dying. My breathing came in shallow gasps. The grips of an imaginary vice squeezed my mind and scrambled my emotions. I ran into the bathroom to throw up. When I looked in the mirror, I couldn't recognize myself. On an emotional scale of one to ten, I was a minus five.

My mind spun like a tilt-a-whirl out of control. An onset of vertigo had me bouncing off the walls. "Is this how it ends, Lord?" I said aloud during a rare instant of lucidity.

I zigzagged to my office, sat down, and tried to breathe deeply. I couldn't. I opened up my Bible, but the words were fuzzy. I begged for mercy; then I prayed for the Lord to take me quickly. The panic came in billows, like huge waves pounding an isolated shore.

In despair, I careened to the sun room and sat in a rocking chair facing north, bent over, my head in my hands, waiting to die. At that point, Molly returned from a trip to the grocery store. She dropped a bag filled with fruit when she saw me sitting there. "What is wrong, Paul? Do you need to go to the emergency room?"

"I don't want to go anywhere. I just want to sit here and die." She ran in alarm to the phone and called Dr. DeAngelo who told her I was having an anxiety attack and wasn't going to die. He called our pharmacy and prescribed a benzodiazepine that would end the attack. When Molly told me the name of the drug, a curious thing happened. It had such a strange name that the sound of it made me feel better.

While the prescription was being prepared, my precious Molly calmly whispered to me. "It will be all right, my darling. The doctor said you will pull out of this." She knelt before my chair and held my hands in hers, with great compassion, not saying another word. My mind and emotions were still spinning, but her hands in mine gave me a sense of grounding.

Within minutes, the phone rang. It was the pharmacy. Molly rushed down and back to pick up the medication. One pill and thirty minutes later the anxiety was gone. I thank the Lord for such a drug. I'm ready to start the next chapter.

✞ ✞ ✞

1992. The third lesson on the same theme arrived in December. There were two parts to it, the first of which occurred one evening as I looked at Christmas decorations across the street. A scene from a Christmas past appeared in my imagination like a movie, starring little Paul at the age of eleven.

Scene One: Early Christmas morning. I'm huddled in the kitchen with my sister and two brothers listening to my first classical composition – Maurice Ravel's *Bolero* – blasting forth in the early morning hours to announce something new was in the house. We're all giggling as our parents come running down the stairs with their hands over their ears, in bewilderment.

On the other side of the kitchen against the dining-room wall stands a console record player, occupying a space where nothing had been the night before. We kids had pooled our money to buy the player for our parents. The record player was my sister's idea, and she was the one who chose *Bolero* as the christening piece, partly because it had a loud ending that would rattle the windows when played at full volume, but mostly because the man who sold her the console threw it in for free.

Scene Two: Listening to *Bolero* one week later. The composition by Ravel fascinated me for reasons I didn't understand as a young boy. I just knew I liked it and wanted to hear it again and again. I am alone, sitting in front of the console, listening to *Bolero*. Everyone else has grown tired of it and annoyed with my listening to it over and over and over again.

Scene Three: Listening to Beethoven's Fifth Symphony seven months later. My taste in classical music had broadened to include works by Beethoven, Bach, and Aaron Copeland. A paper route I started in January and caddying at the golf course gave me the wherewithal to expand my classical collection. I look at the little bookcase my father gave me to hold my records. One shelf is full.

After watching the three scenes, I put the movie into its storage place in my memory, not knowing another drama, soon to be played out, would be the second installment of the third lesson.

I had related the Life 21 story to my friend Pastor Bruce during a November get-together in Willmar. He suggested I visit North Central University in Minneapolis and talk to Larry Bach, the Dean of the College of Fine Arts. "I think there's more to this story than meets the eye. Maybe Larry can help you."

"Help me with what?" Bruce had a way of coming up with proclamations that sounded like prophecies. Oftentimes they were.

"I really don't know for sure," he answered. "Maybe it has something to do with the idea of an under melody playing alongside the melody of this world."

Professor Bach wanted to put off any meeting until January, after the beginning of the next semester. I pushed him a bit because Pastor Bruce's foresight energized my thinking. He finally agreed to a short visit two weeks before Christmas. I drove from my home in Willmar to Minneapolis in less than two hours, but it took another hour to find the college tucked into a maze of streets near Loring Park, discover the right building and an unlocked door, and track down Professor Bach's office. I was afraid I'd be late for our meeting.

As I stood in an office corridor that had no names announcing who lived where, I noticed a line of students waiting outside a door, the ones at the end sitting on the floor. "Could you tell me where Professor Bach's office is?"

One of the girls thought that a funny question. "You're standing in front of it. We're all waiting for him to sign off on our schedules for next semester."

I knocked on the door and the professor opened it with a welcoming smile on his face. "You must be Paul Chambers." I nodded. "As you can see, I have a long line of advisees waiting to see me. I can give you ten minutes."

I skipped the pleasantries and explained the music I'd heard July 12 in Northfield. I remember his smiling like someone who'd been asked what day it was. "What you heard is called counterpoint or counter melody, the playing of one melody at the same time as another. It's used in classical music and also vocal music, including praise and worship songs. A good example of counterpoint," he continued, "is *Bolero*, written by Maurice Ravel in 1928."

I left North Central University with a sense of wonderment. A fresh blanket of snow was beginning to fall as I walked to my car, lost in thought. A musical composition I'd first heard at the age of eleven had just attached itself to a unique rendering of *Jesus, Lover of my Soul*. I felt the snow falling against my face and a blanket of it underneath my feet. In a voice that could only have been heard by a person walking alongside me, I prayed, "My life is a tapestry woven by You, Lord. How marvelous You are! You have connected a movie from my earliest years to an event You directed last July in Northfield and now to my discussion with Professor Bach."

The drive back home from Minneapolis was serene. The snow fell softly all the way, enough to transform the landscape into a Christmas morning in Bethlehem but not enough to make the roads slippery. Only a few cars traveled the same highway, no more than four or five a mile. It was as if I were driving in a different world.

The first thing I did upon entering my home was to turn on the computer and type "counterpoint" into *Search*. I wrote this definition in my journal: "A counter melody, also known as a counterpoint, is a secondary melody played simultaneously with the main melody but independent of it." I listened to *Bolero* with a fresh mindset. My next journal entry was two weeks later, having listened to Ravel's composition at least once a day during that time.

A flute announces the alluring main melody, followed shortly after by the soft sound of two snare drums introducing the counter melody.

As the music progresses, an oboe, bassoon, and other wind instruments bolster the main melody. Plucked violas, cellos, and a harp reinforce the counter melody, which gradually becomes louder and more distinct, until reaching a crescendo at the end.

You have shown me, Holy Spirit, that the counterpoint in Bolero is a metaphor for my relationship with You. Before my salvation, I could hear only the seductive song of the world and the disharmony of my natural self. Now I hear Your melody as a counterpoint, and it grows louder and louder until I hear it distinctly much of the time.

The sermon in Fargo. The Holy Spirit empowered hymn in Northfield. The listening to *Bolero* as a young boy and the meeting with Larry Bach in Minneapolis. I had no doubt who had orchestrated these connections, but didn't realize at the time there were more transformational lessons to come from God's classroom. The Holy Spirit would be waiting for me at the same church in Northfield ten years later for another critical lesson.

3

Monday, November 7, 2011. Another panic attack knocked on my door this morning. I felt a twinge in my stomach and a pinch in my brain, just like I did last Friday. Molly peeked her head into the door of the office. "You had better take another benzodiazepine before panic sets in again."

"Is my anxiety that noticeable?"

"Your eyes look similar to Friday, and your face is pale. When you asked if your anxiety was noticeable, your voice cracked."

"Thanks for noticing, Molly. I think you're right" I took a pill from a bottle on my desk and swallowed it without water. I started feeling better immediately, remembering the results of two days ago. I'm ready to write.

✞ ✞ ✞

1993. Nine months after the meeting with Larry Bach. I was immersed in the Holy Spirit as a result of the three lessons of 1992. It was Holy Spirit this and Holy Spirit that. I was too enthused to notice listeners' eyes glazing over when I told them of His wonders.

One evening at the dinner table, Molly looked down at her food and said in a non-judgmental way, "I fear you may be going too far with the Holy Spirit."

I threw my hands up defensively, "Whoa! How can anyone go too far with the Holy Spirit?" I didn't mean to be irritable, but I was.

Molly didn't have an unkind bone in her body. Normally, she would have backed off, but not this time. She held her ground. "The French have a saying: 'The faults lie in the virtues.'"

"Why'd you bring that up?" I was still playing defense, still petulant, and not very lovable. Molly retreated from the argument with one comment.

"You are playing golf with Neil tomorrow. Ask him if you are going overboard with the Holy Spirit." It was quiet the rest of the evening.

My favorite golf partner was Dr. Neil Johnson, a long-time friend and fellow member of a Bible study that lasted fifteen years. He didn't dress like a golfer, nor did he look like a golfer. Everything about him was round – a round head on a round body on round legs. He looked like a snowman.

We met in the parking lot and were soon standing on the first tee. It was a cool morning, and Neil was wearing tennis shoes, baggy pants, and an old sweatshirt. On his head was a floppy hat you see on someone tending a garden. But I loved him for what he was on the inside, not how he looked on the outside. He was one of my best friends, only a notch below my brother Teddy.

Following a so-so front nine for both of us, I steered our conversation to my favorite subject: the influence of the Holy Spirit in our lives. Neil was a deep-thinking Christ-follower; I thought he would provide me with a good argument to bring back to Molly. I didn't think I was going overboard with the Holy Spirit.

As we stepped off the tenth green, I posed a question: "Neil, the Holy Spirit has been the featured attraction in my spiritual walk lately. Molly thinks I may be going too far, but I don't think so. How can anyone go too far with the Holy Spirit?"

"What do you say the purpose of the Holy Spirit is?" asked Neil, as he slammed his putter into his golf bag and jumped into the cart. He had just missed a three-foot putt.

"Do you want to discuss it now or wait until you cool down?"

Neil shook his head. "I don't know why I let a golf game get the best of me. I'm ready to hear your response."

The eleventh tee box was a hundred yards away. I drove as fast as the cart would go and slammed the brakes on before we slammed into a ball washer. I turned to Neil with my answer. His hands were on the front of the cart bracing for a crash. "To guide and teach me. To convict me of sin and show me how to pray rightly. To be my counselor and help me in my weakness."

"If you did that race-track stunt to make me forget about that lousy putt, you've succeeded." I smiled as he continued. "You've listed important components of His work, but you've left out the most important one."

We were on the tee box at the time and ready to navigate the most difficult hole on the course. There was out of bounds to the right, woods on the left, and a nasty dog-leg that crossed a deep ravine. It demanded a nearly perfect drive. We both kept our tee shots in play, one of the few times that happened on the eleventh hole.

On the way to our second shots, I asked, "What am I missing?"

"Well, you hit your drive right down the middle, but you could have gained more distance if you had cut the dog-leg."

"Funny, funny. I wasn't talking about my golf game."

He put his hand to his face in a Jack Benny manner and said, "Well, what do you know? All right, as you wish, let's get serious. The main purpose of the Holy Spirit is to lead us to Jesus. And our main purpose is to glorify Jesus through the power of the Holy Spirit and to love people. Jesus tells us in the 15th and 16th chapters of John that the Holy Spirit 'will testify about me' and 'will bring glory to me by taking from what is mine and making it known to you.' You've been keeping the Holy Spirit to yourself, my friend, and that creates a problem. He's the fresh spring water that feeds your soul so you can be an outlet to others and tell them about Jesus."

We each reached the difficult-to-hit green on our second shots, the only time that happened. I shook my head as we rolled along in the golf cart. "I know that and I've reached out in love to my family, friends, and people in prisons and nursing homes for the past year, ever since the sermon in Fargo I told you about. Are you're telling me I'm too much like Bad Medicine Lake in northern Minnesota?"

"Where did you fetch that from?" said Neil. "I've heard of Bad Medicine, but what does it have to do with our conversation?"

"It has a lot to do with it. The Indians in Becker County, where I grew up, gave the name to the lake because it was spring fed with no outlets. They felt it was bad medicine. Get it? It's the picture you're painting of me – fed by the Holy Spirit but holding it all in. Isn't that what you're telling me?"

Neil nodded his head up and down. "That's exactly what I'm telling you. Do *you* get it? Doing things for Christ is one thing. Doing things through Him is much better. Advancing His kingdom by telling others about Him is best. It's the second request in the Lord's Prayer: 'Thy kingdom come.' How can His kingdom come without your being used by Christ to help in the process? It's the Great Commission: 'Therefore go and make disciples of all nations.' Who will go if you don't?" The good doctor had gone into his preaching mode.

"OK. I get it. You've convicted me. Are you happy now?" But he wasn't the one doing the convicting: it was the Holy Spirit through him.

"I *am* happy now, delighted in fact, absolutely ecstatic. You have seen the light. Praise the Lord, you've seen the light. Hallelujah!"

"Your sarcasm is not becoming of you," I said with a slight smile. "By the way, I just thought of a better example than Bad Medicine Lake."

"The lake was just starting to make sense and now you're going to introduce something new. Give me a break."

"Don't panic. It isn't that complicated," I said with a hearty laugh. "Bad Medicine Lake never changes. It is what it is all the time. My state of being is more fluid. What you're saying about the Holy Spirit is resonating within me. My wife said much the same thing yesterday evening. Say, did she call you up this morning?"

"No, she didn't call me up this morning. Your paranoia is getting the best of you."

"I'm not paranoid. I just think everyone is out to get me." Neil gave me a quizzical look. "Just kidding," I added.

"All right, let me hear your better example."

"You'll like it, I'm sure. My golf swing is a more accurate illustration. Sometimes it's very good; other times it's less than adequate. My spiritual disposition is similar. Sometimes everything falls into place, and I'm an obedient servant. Other times the spiritual pieces don't fit together, and I lose track of what it means to be a Christian. Carrying the Holy Spirit to an extreme was the result of losing my spiritual moorings. It's like hitting a golf ball from the wrong angle, resulting in a wicked slice. It's troubling I neither have my best swing all the time nor do I have all of Christ all the time."

"Don't be too hard on yourself," said Neil, as the cart rolled down the fairway. "I've seen your steady growth as a Christian, but few of us plod along smoothly without bumps in the road. Being a Christian *is* hard. It was never meant to be easy. We need constant encouragement and reminders: that's the purpose of Christian fellowship. Consider yourself reminded."

"Thanks, Neil. You do an admirable job of that."

"My pleasure," he responded, with a silly grin on his face.

We parked the cart and walked to the green. Neil made a snaky twenty-foot putt on a downslope that would have gone off the green had he missed. I had a ten-foot uphill putt that went straight in. It was the first time on any hole on any course we had both made birdie.

4

Tuesday, November 8, 2011. An unfamiliar face greeted me this morning in the bathroom mirror. A face with a hint of yellow and eyes with a slight golden glow stared back. I had seen hints of it before but thought it was a glow from the overhead lights. I moved closer. It was unmistakable, not decidedly distinctive but clearly detectable. Tears glistened on my face. "Oh, Lord, have mercy on me," I said over and over. My legs were shaky as I arose and left the bathroom.

Molly was in the laundry room, putting clothes in the washer. I told her what I'd seen and she replied, "I know, Paul, I've been watching it develop for the past week."

"Why didn't you say anything to me?" I asked with a childlike voice, pulling her close to me, with one hand behind her head as if to steady myself.

She stuttered, "I th-thought you did not want to talk about it."

I had no response. We moved into the living room and sat on the couch in silence, hands intertwined and heads bowed. We both cried, but no words were spoken. What could we say? It will only get worse.

A gloomy thought entered my mind as I walked into the office to start writing. "This yellowness is a mask of death, a constant reminder the end is approaching. If I don't block out that image, it will consume me."

✞ ✞ ✞

1997. With the dark thought of the mask of death shoved into the cellar of my soul, I will jump ahead four years, back on the same golf course with Neil.

Neil was an average golfer but a remarkable fellow other than that. He was known by his friends as a Renaissance man – someone accomplished in many subjects. He was an outstanding internist who knew the *American Medical Association Complete Medical Encyclopedia* almost by heart. Most doctors need to step outside their office on occasion to look up the symptoms of a disease in a medical book. Dr. Neil Johnson never did, not for uncommon afflictions, not even for rare diseases.

He broadened out from there. He was an investing guru in stocks, bonds, closed-end funds, hedge funds, and commodity futures. For a few years, he entered a national commodities contest to see who could amass the greatest gains with a $50,000 common stake. He won every year but one.

Neil was also a bird watcher who had a count of more than five thousand birds worldwide. And when he stepped on a car lot, he knew more about any car than even the most knowledgeable salesperson.

However, his greatest gift was his knowledge and understanding of the Bible. He was a regular Sunday-school teacher and presenter who filled any size room the church put him in. And more than once he stood in the pulpit for a vacationing pastor. It was this talent I wanted to tap into.

To have more of God in my life more of the time, I needed a better understanding of how He interacts with His children. I understood to the degree I could how my spirit and soul mixed together to govern my thoughts and behavior, but how did my heart fit into the equation? There was a phrase I'd used myself when leading unbelievers into God's kingdom: "Do you accept Jesus Christ into your heart?" What did that *really* mean? Neil would know. Neil knew everything.

The course we were on had few players that day. For me, the round was a get-together with a good friend, and it was for Neil as well, along with an additional goal. He wanted to shoot the lower score, which rarely happened, maybe once or twice every three years.

Cumulus clouds and blue sky were taking turns covering up and displaying a brilliant sun. The lilacs bordering the fairways smelled fresh and clean and sweet and innocent, in a perfect state for presentation to mothers the next Sunday. I posed a question to Neil as we stepped off the third tee. "Oh, learned doctor, I need your wisdom to explain something I'm having trouble grasping."

"Such flattery. Do you want to borrow money?" He laughed heartily.

"Well, no, but if you have a couple extra bucks, I'd me happy to take them off your hands. Seriously, what I really want is your explanation on something I'm having trouble with. What, Dr. Johnson, is the heart of man? And I'm not referring to the physical heart."

"That I could have answered in one minute. What, dear fellow, are you wanting?" He grinned in a way only he could, like the Cheshire cat in *Alice's Adventures in Wonderland*. And, like the famous cat, he could raise philosophical questions that baffled me. Or he could explain spiritual matters no one else could touch. He was my best bet for understanding the heart of man.

"I can sense God in my spirit though I can't see Him or touch Him," I said. "And I can observe how souls interact with the world and each other, but the heart of man confounds me. The dictionary's not much help. How can you sort out fifty definitions? And the Bible's downright confusing, with over five-hundred citations that differ from slightly to greatly. Most learned scholar, I know you could speak on the matter for the entire round, but my head would be spinning. I'd like to offer you a challenge. If you can define the non-physical heart in one sentence, I'll spot you ten strokes the next time we play."

"I can't refuse that offer," said Neil with great enthusiasm. "Ten strokes! You wouldn't have a chance to beat me. How long do I have?"

"How about by the end of the round?"

"You're crazy, you know. I don't have the answer at the top of my mind. I need to do some research."

"OK," I responded. "How about one week?"

"Done. I'll give you one clue to think about in the meantime: the heart is a metaphor, not an actual entity like spirit and soul."

The next discussion topic was Neil's success with investing in hedge funds, which lasted five holes. By the time we finished the round, we had discussed *The Seven Habits of Highly Effective People*, the 1918 Migratory Bird Act, and several theological arguments for the existence of God – and set a date for breakfast at Bixby's in exactly one week.

I walked into Bixby's seven days later and saw Neil sitting at a table with his notebook and Bible. The two front pockets of his shirt were stuffed with 3 by 5 cards. The left pocket was his *in* basket and the right one his *out* basket. It was an organizational system put in place before the advent of electronic planners and smartphones. "He looks like he's ready," I thought as I sat down. Neil was a get-to-the-point kind of guy and not big on the art of gushy hellos and small talk. He dove straight into the subject at hand as soon as we had our coffee and ordered.

"Well, Paul, I came up with a one-sentence definition of heart, but it wasn't easy. I had five sentences in place in thirty minutes and narrowed it down to three in another hour, but it took three hours to refine it down to a single sentence."

"Let's hear it."

"Not so fast. I want to share with you some of the research I did along the way."

I took a sip of coffee and settled in to listen to a doctoral thesis.

Neil opened his Bible and read from Mark 12:30: "'Love the Lord your God with all your heart and with all your soul and with all your mind and with all your strength.' This verse tells me the heart is something different than the body or soul, and nothing I've found in Scripture indicates that the heart and spirit are the same thing."

Neil next turned to John 5:42 and read what Jesus said to His persecutors, "'I know you. I know that you do not have the love of God in your hearts.' Though not said directly, I think Jesus is saying that these hypocrites had the love of themselves and the world in their hearts instead." Neil had markers stuck in his Bible, another of his idiosyncrasies, so he was able to turn quickly to Matthew 5:8. "Jesus further pictured those whose hearts were filled with God when he told his disciples, 'Blessed are the pure in heart, for they will see God.'"

I put on a face of impatience and tapped my fingers on the table. I smiled in my subdued way, not at all like the Cheshire Cat. "I'm waiting for the one-sentence definition, s'il vous plait."

"Well aren't you the cosmopolitan one, using the French for please?" He wagged his head when he said this – his way of poking fun at me.

"Let me add one more piece and then I'll be done." Neil chuckled because he knew full well his reputation to explain something far beyond anyone's need to know. "I find Luke 6:45 an interesting verse, where Jesus pictures the heart as being like a storage container. 'A good man brings good things out of the good stored up in his heart, and an evil man brings evil things out of the evil stored up in his heart.' Now I'm done."

"Praise the Lord," I said and threw my hands up in the air as an act of jubilation. That set him back in his chair because I was rarely so demonstrative. "*Now* for the definition!"

Just then the food arrived. "I'll tell you when we've finished breakfast."

I shook my head back and forth. "You've done it again. If you're given a five-pound bag to explain something, you stuff it with ten pounds." We laughed at that picture, said grace, and disposed of our food.

When we each finished the last morsel and pushed away the plates, Neil said, "Take your notebook out, Paul, and write down this definition. Your challenge was for one sentence; here it is.

> The heart is the center of our total personality, the repository of our deepest and sincerest feelings and beliefs, the storehouse of our values, and the source of our motivation and emotions.

5

Tuesday Afternoon, November 8, 2011. The sun is at high noon, and I'm still in my pajamas. It took all morning to write the last chapter. I'm exhausted, but it's a good exhaustion. Writing helps keep my mind off my condition.

Molly and I ate lunch together, as we have for many years, beginning with our courting days at the college. It's been our way of coming together during busy days. Why Pete came to mind I don't know, perhaps because he also had cancer.

"Do you remember my friend Pete, Molly?"

"Very well. He was the best golf partner you ever had. Why are you bringing him up?"

"I'm not sure. I was looking at my sandwich and saw his face. He loved tuna fish. The doctors pronounced him cancer-free during the Christmas season of 1996. Then a perforated ulcer welcomed him into the new year and took his life."

"Are you making a connection between his situation and yours?" Molly asked.

"I guess I am. Dr. Ferrington told me my prostate cancer was under control and ten months later Dr. DeAngelo announced I had pancreatic cancer. That's a pretty close correlation. But more to the point, Pete's death grieved me for a reason different than losing a golf buddy."

"I think I know why but tell me."

"He wasn't a churchgoer and gave no hints of being a Christian. I tried to lure him with my salvation story and what God means to me, but he never bit. I became more direct when he was diagnosed with melanoma, but he'd have none of it. I should have pushed harder, done everything I could, left no stone unturned."

"You did everything you could. He did not want anything to do with Jesus."

"I don't think I did everything I could. And where is he now? I shudder to think of it."

"Let us change the subject to something more pleasant. Discussing Pete is a downer for you. Did you finally finish the chapter of your book you were working on this morning?"

"I did, and I'm about to write one more chapter."

"I do not think that is a good idea, Paul. Dr. DeAngelo said you should not overdo it."

"And he's right. I agree with you. But this next chapter isn't going to be a burden. I'm going to copy it word for word out of my 1997 journal. Do you want to hear it first? You might find it amusing because you're included in the beginning."

"You have piqued my interest. Please read it to me."

I opened up my journal to the 1997 section and read the entry slowly.

✝ ✝ ✝

1997. "I'd appreciate it if you don't ask me to do anything else today," I told Molly this morning as I walked into my office to spend an hour with the Lord.

"Are you going to spend all day in prayer?" she asked.

"No. Not that. I already have ten items on my to-do list that have to get done today."

"I will not burden you with more. May the Lord bless you today and help you accomplish your agenda. Do leave room in your schedule for me tomorrow."

"I will," I answered with a pang of guilt. "I promise."

My mind was as still as the weather outside, as I observed a glazing of ice on the windows. "Be with me, Lord, through the busyness of this day." As I prayed, I heard the Lord's voice, not with audible words but with a clear thought.

"You ask Me to fit into your agenda instead of asking Me how you might fit into Mine."

He convicted me because His thought arrived with authority and truth. I saw pictures in my mind of times I'd asked Jesus to be with me in this or that situation, as if He were a tag-along. I remember one time in particular in the late 1980s when I asked Jesus to be with me before meeting with a problem instructor and her union representative. The Holy Spirit imparted this thought to me then: "You are wrong in your thinking. Jesus is always with you. The point is whether you are always with Him?"

I walked to the window of my office and smiled as I watched a person across the street, dressed like an Eskimo, shoveling his driveway. He slipped on some ice and went down hard but seemed unhurt because he was so bundled up.

Once I saw he was OK, my mind went back to the problem instructor and her union rep. I learned a valuable lesson that day as I sat in the conference room waiting for those two to arrive. I had dumbly requested Jesus to be with me because it's what I'd heard others say.

I asked the Holy Spirit for an explanation, and it was forthcoming in a quiet whisper kind of way, not to my outer ear but to my inner one. It's hard to explain. Those who have heard from the Lord know what I'm talking about.

"It's not what you're doing but where you're standing when you do it." I was perplexed. I'd never have thought that on my own, so I was quite sure the Spirit was leading me.

I remember the union guy had been caught in traffic on the way out, so I had fifteen minutes I wouldn't have had otherwise. As I was waiting, the Holy Spirit placed two images into my imagination. Both took place on a thrust stage, like at the Guthrie Theater in downtown Minneapolis. It was almost an exact repeat of the images He had given me ten years earlier on the golf course in Ellendale, North Dakota, except these were sharper and more brilliant. It was like a black and white movie that had been reshot in full color.

In the first image, I am standing at the front of the stage as the main actor, with Jesus and everyone else playing supporting roles. In the second image, Jesus is standing at the front of the stage, with me and everyone else standing behind as supporting actors.

I remember thinking at the time, "The Holy Spirit must have given me this vision a second time because I was too slow on the uptake to live it out the first time." Just then the door opened and the two walked in. It was a fruitful meeting because I was standing behind Jesus, letting him play the lead role.

I put on a warm sweater and my super-insulated parka. The man across the street was limping. Aiding the shoveler was not on my busy agenda, but what else could I do? As I headed out the door, I thought, "When I'm at the front of the stage, I ask Jesus to help me accomplish my agenda. With Jesus front and center, I ask Him how I can help accomplish His agenda, things both large and small, like helping a limping shoveler."

When I finished the reading, Molly said to me, "Thank you for sharing that with me. Was the limping shoveler Ron from across the street?"

"It was. His wife had banged his leg when she threw open her car door the day before while he was standing too close to it."

6

Wednesday, November 16, 2011. Joe is still single and living in Minneapolis, but his marital status is about to change. Molly and I spent the weekend with him and met his fiancée, a young lady named Celine. She has long black hair and a natural look without much makeup. The way they looked at each other, it was obvious they were in love.

Joe winced when he saw me coming through his back door; Celine turned her eyes away. He hadn't seen my mask of death before. The yellow pallor wasn't arresting; but the last time we were together, my complexion was still a deep tan from playing golf all summer. I don't think Celine expected to see someone who looked like he had a foot in the grave. She tried to appear unaffected but couldn't hide her uneasiness. She was careful with the words she used and as a result didn't use many of them. After supper, I asked Joe if we could go down in the basement so I could give him a lesson on golf.

"I really don't want to talk to you about golf, Joe," I said as we stood in the basement.

"I didn't think so." He awaited my next line.

"I can see my condition is troubling you and Celine. I don't want us to continue on that way. I'm not feeling as bad as I look."

"Dad, Celine and I have talked about moving our wedding date ahead from next fall to this coming spring." I didn't have to ask why they wanted to do that.

"No, Joe, don't do it. This is your wedding and your life together, not mine. Stay with the timetable you two have set. Who knows? I may be walking up the aisle with Mom next October. Just to let you know how well I'm doing, let's play golf tomorrow. I'll bet I beat you by five strokes." That relaxed Joe a bit.

"I'd like that, Dad. What's the wager?"

"If I win, you'll stop worrying about me and pay attention to your bride-to-be and your upcoming wedding."

"And what if I win?"

"That isn't going to happen."

Joe took Monday off work for our round of golf. It was an unusually warm day for November, twenty-five degrees above average. I realized during the round that this would be another last-time event, so I might as well give it all I had. I didn't have my usual length on drives and irons, but my chipping and putting were stellar. I shot a 78 and my healthy, muscular son shot an 85. I won the bet.

As we sat in the clubhouse having a soda, I said to Joe, "Well, son, you can see I'm not gone yet. Now stop worrying about me and get on with your own life."

"I will, Dad." He had a relieved smile on his face. For him, 85 was the best score he'd shot in a couple of years, so it wasn't that he let me win. I was still the golf champion of the Chambers family.

✝ ✝ ✝

1998. The chapters of my book are like a toggle switch. I first tell what's happening to me in the present with pancreatic cancer. Then I flip the switch to the past and write out of my memory, aided by my highlights journal. I can only write so much about the present before needing to flip to the relief of the past. The one is filled with anguish; the other with joyful memories.

Today's flip of the switch brings me back to the summer and fall of 1998. I was rolling along with more of God in my life more of the time when a sudden crisis struck my mother and threatened my spiritual well-being.

She was having trouble eating solid foods, so much so that the nursing staff was afraid she'd choke to death. It ended up to be esophageal cancer. No one loved me as she did. To lose her was unthinkable. I argued with God to let her live, not a humble prayer but a demand.

Non-Christian colleagues at the college were more than willing to challenge my faith. A welding instructor said to me, not in a nasty way but with skepticism. "You've told me God is good all the time. I'm very sorry for your mother's sickness, but I can't see how it's a good thing."

I couldn't answer him. I didn't think it was a good thing either. My faith was shaken.

I began visiting her twice a month instead of once, and then weekly. The trip from our house to the nursing home in Hankinson, North Dakota and back was five hours all together. I was emotionally paralyzed when I imagined my world without her in it. I agonized. I became depressed. It was all about me. How would I go on? Trusting in the Lord was below ground level, about ten feet down.

In my despondency, I saw Him as a great watchmaker in heaven who had wound up the clock of earth and watched it tick, tick, tick, without being personally involved with the troubles of His people. One morning as I prayed for relief, the Comforter put into my mind the metaphor of a compass. No words, just a compass.

I learned the value of a compass as a Boy Scout at Wilderness Camp. Scoutmasters led three other boys and me into a dense forest and told us to find our way out, with only a compass to guide us. Without that compass showing us true north, we'd be shamefully rescued at the end of the day and not awarded a merit badge.

But that wasn't the compass the Holy Spirit showed me. The one in my imagination had God at the North Pole and me at the South Pole. He was True North, and I was floundering about in the southern hemisphere, paying more attention to my predicament than to Him. I grabbed my journal as the truth flooded into me.

We know how to align ourselves with true north on a compass, but how do we align ourselves with the True North of God? The simple answer is we can't, any more than we can perform heart surgery on ourselves. We need the Holy Spirit to be our guide and point us in the right direction.

Believers face True North when they earnestly listen to the Holy Spirit, but spiritual feet are prone to wander. As we walk to the east or west less than 90 degrees, we're still in God's hemisphere, but when we wander more than 90 degrees either way, we're in the southern hemisphere, drawn to the world and our own self-centered self. Holy Spirit, push me back into the northern hemisphere.

I experienced great sorrow as the cancer in my mother's body sapped her vitality. So vibrant to me when I was growing up, she was now wasting away before my eyes. One night, as she was sleeping in a nursing home in Hankinson, North Dakota, I prayed for her without words in my own bed, one-hundred-and-twenty miles away. In my imagination, I knelt by the side of her bed as she slept. Looking up, I saw a gleaming cross above her head, knowing from many visits there that the cross would be pointing to true north on a standard compass. I saw it as also pointing to True North on God's compass. The cross glowed with a warm white light, and I was heartened that my mother's soul was aligned with God. I fell asleep knowing Mom was doing absolutely fine and would soon be with her Lord and Savior.

A month later, she had a stroke and went into a deep unconsciousness. Her living will dictated that in case of a coma, she was not to be given food or water. I stayed in a room at the nursing home for three days. On the third night, I was awakened from a sound sleep by a nurse who told me Mother was gone. I went into her room and held her in my arms peacefully until the undertaker arrived, keeping a watchful eye on the cross at the head of her bed. God was merciful to take her in that manner. My faith was restored.

7

Thursday, November 17, 2011. Last Monday's golf outing resulted in a two-stroke penalty. On Tuesday and Wednesday, the pain in my back jumped from a 5 to a 10, which tortured my body like a merciless fiend. The other penalty was two sleepless nights. The combination put me on the phone with Dr. DeAngelo yesterday afternoon.

"Have you taken the morphine I prescribed?"

"No, I didn't want my mind to be affected by narcotics. The benzodiazepines I took did not dull my thinking. But morphine is a much different animal."

"Are you having a good time now?" He had fallen into sarcasm instead of his usual friendliness.

"Would I be calling you if I were?" I said with a snipe of my own.

"The pain in your back and your sleeplessness aren't going to go away. I don't mean to be a hard-ass, but don't give me another call until you start taking the morphine." There was no joking in his voice.

I hung up the phone and took my first dose. The deep, steady pain abated markedly but my thinking became wobbly. I slept well last night and am more clear headed this morning.

"How did you sleep last night?" asked Molly from under the blankets when I stepped out of bed.

"Very well, and my mind isn't foggy this morning. I'm ready to continue on with the story."

"That is good," she said with sleep still in her voice.

✛ ✛ ✛

2002. After Mom's passing, I returned to experiencing more of God more of the time on a regular basis for the next four years. It was like breathing out and breathing in.

Molly and I had taken early retirement from the college and moved from Willmar to Buffalo, Minnesota to be an hour closer to our two boys. Molly was content to walk away from a career of thirty-five years. Jack and Catherine had a baby named Margo, and Molly took great delight in being her Nana. I was not content with retirement and started a new career as a professional business coach.

I was pleased with my spiritual journey of more of God more of the time. But God wasn't. He didn't want more of my time; He wanted all of it. I read the Bible more often, prayed more often, was aware of His presence in my life more often, and spoke to others about Him more often. All that moved me closer to that part of my spiritual path where I would experience more of God most of the time, but I was not yet there. As to experiencing more of God all of the time, I suspected that wouldn't happen until I was with Him in eternity.

I had become wiser by this time and knew I couldn't reach my spiritual goal by what I thought or what I did. I needed the Holy Spirit to charge my soul with a burst of high-voltage electricity to launch me a few miles further down the road. I prayed for a mountaintop experience. I had no idea what that might be but trusted He did. A defining encounter happened at Life 21 Church in Northfield, in the cloak of a remarkable vision.

Molly and I drove seventy-five miles through light snow and arrived in Northfield on a Friday evening to take care of Margo. Her parents left early Saturday morning to visit friends in St. Paul. Margo developed a slight fever Saturday evening but was much better Sunday morning. However, Molly didn't feel she should go outside into the cold air, so I went off to church by myself.

The sky was an airy white without a break of blue as I drove to the church. I was looking forward to the service at Life 21, my church home away from Buffalo.

As I walked into the front foyer of the church, I remember yawning. My friend Gary saw it and stepped up to me, his nose one foot from mine. "You need a jolt from the Holy Spirit this morning, Paul. You need a jolt from the Holy Spirit!" As he walked away, I had a supernatural feeling that something monumental was about to happen.

All services I attended at Life 21 began the same way: impromptu personal testimonies followed by praise and worship music. This day was different. Pastor Lew walked in slow motion up the middle aisle and stood quietly before the altar for at least a minute. No one knew what was about to happen, not even Pastor Lew. As he had once said to the congregation, "I don't run this service; the Holy Spirit does."

He turned to face the congregation and requested in a soft voice I'd never heard him use before: "For those who can, please go to your knees and silently pray to forget yourselves and the things of this world and prepare to worship the living God." That's all he said.

I knelt and began to pray mindlessly: "Lord, I ask that You help me forget about myself and the things of this world," and continued on in that fashion. The Holy Spirit was not impressed with such a lifeless prayer and turned my mind to an inward vision. In my imagination, I saw a radio with a manual-tuning dial and an FM broadcast frequency band that had stations on either end.

World/Self Station		*Holy Spirit Station*
87.7 fm	*97.9 fm*	*107.9 fm*

As I looked inward at the radio dial, I asked the Holy Spirit for clarification. He explained that one end of the radio band played the values of the world and the inclinations of my natural self and the other played God's values and His love for me.

I remember feeling excited with this epiphany and launched a new prayer. "Lord, push me away from the World/Self Station that is interfering with my listening to you most of the time. Draw me closer to Your Holy Spirit Station." As if in a dream, I turned the dial from the middle frequencies I had been hearing to a higher frequency. It was so real I could see my hand turning the frequency knob. The congregation remained in silent prayer for five minutes; then the testimonies began.

Something wonderful had come to pass. I knew it. The mountaintop experience I was praying for materialized out of thin air. I could feel a tingling in my body, and a spotlight lit up my mind, will, and emotions. I remember it now as if it happened two hours ago.

My head was in the clouds as I drove back to my son's home, as wisps of snow were starting to fall. That evening, back home in Buffalo, I warmed myself before the lower-level fireplace and gazed at the flames, lost in the Holy Spirit. I wrote this entry in my journal without effort on my part:

> The signal of the Holy Spirit Station can be heard along the entire frequency band, but the strength of its signal is strongest the closer a believer is tuned toward 107.9 and weakest the nearer 87.7. In the same way, the signal of the World/Self Station can be heard along the entire frequency band, but the strength of its signal is strongest the closer one is tuned toward 87.7 and weakest the nearer 107.9. The music of the world/self is always present within a believer, and so too the melody of the Holy Spirit. The place where the two signals are of equal strength is 97.9.
>
> There are two choices ever before me. Do I tune to the World/Self Station and hear a little interference from the Holy Spirit Station? Or do I tune to the melody of the Holy Spirit with a trace of static from the World/Self frequency? I can barely hear the voice of God when I'm focused on myself and the things of this world, but I hear Him clearly when I'm in tune with the Holy Spirit.

Sometimes you recognize a few years later that an encounter with God was a major development in your life. Sometimes you recognize it immediately. This was of the immediate variety and ranked right up there with the under melody sequence of lessons from ten years prior.

I could hardly wait to share my interior radio metaphor with my friend Ben who lived on a farm outside Buffalo. I first met him at a farm conference held at our college years back, and we bonded like Christian magnets, getting together once a month until we moved to Buffalo, after which we met weekly. I thought he would share my excitement and marvel at God's involvement in my life. It didn't work out quite that way.

8

2002. Every believer could benefit from having a spiritual partner. Bennett MacDonald was mine, and an odd pair we were. I was six feet tall and weighed 175 pounds, neither too heavy nor too slim. Ben was three inches shorter and weighed 220 pounds, without an ounce of fat. We met in a coffee shop in Buffalo the morning after I returned from Northfield.

Ben was already there, sitting before the fireplace with coffee in hand when I came through the front door. I said hello and walked up to the counter to order what I always ordered – a tall cup of dark roast with cream and sugar. "Well, you look excited this morning, Paul," said Ben, as I dropped down on a leather chair opposite his. "What's up?"

"I'll tell you what's up," I said loudly with great enthusiasm. Curious heads turned at the tables near us, and Ben gave me a tamping-down signal to lower my voice.

"Calm down," he said, "unless you wanna be a preacher addressin your congregation."

I lowered my voice. "Do you remember my telling you about the sermon in Fargo ten years ago, and the under melody hymn in Northfield and meeting with Professor Larry Bach that followed in quick succession?"

"I sure do. You said it was the most important experience of your life, other than your salvation. Is that why you're all excited?"

"No. I brought that up as a reference to the second most important experience in my life – what happened to me last Sunday."

"Weren't you in Northfield?"

"Yes, and I went to a service at Life 21 Church." I proceeded to tell Ben all the details of the vision but noticed he was not nearly as excited as I was.

"I kinda get what you're talkin about, but I'm waitin for you to tell me how that plays out in the real world." I felt like a balloon being deflated. I've since realized visions are personal things and not easily transferrable to someone else.

"OK, Ben," I said in a more subdued voice. "When you are in tune with the Holy Spirit, you're more focused on God, and when you are not in tune, you're more focused on the world and yourself."

"I git that, but I'm still waitin for the answer to my question, 'What's it look like in the real world?' I don't wanta know what it's about; I wanta know what it is."

"Are you asking for a dictionary definition?"

"I'm askin for a practical definition. How do I listen to this melody of the Holy Spirit you're talkin about? How does anyone?"

"Let me freshen up my coffee and I'll answer your question." Fortunately, there was a long line at the counter, and I had time to pray about Ben's question and listen for thoughts from the Holy Spirit.

When I returned to the chair in front of the fireplace, I put the cup down on a small table and rubbed my hands together, speaking slowly and respectfully. "The melody coming from the Holy Spirit Station includes his gifts to us, such as wisdom, understanding, knowledge, and counsel."

"Another gift is the fear of the Lord," Ben added. "Now where do we go?"

"The purpose of the Holy Spirit is not to exalt Himself. He is the teacher who tells us about Jesus and the Father. If you think of it in musical terms – His melody is the harmony of Jesus Christ and the rhythm of God the Father."

"It's makin sense. Keep goin."

"The lyrics of the melody include the words of Scripture and the still, small voice that speaks into the souls of those who are in tune with God. When I'm listening for the melody of the Holy Spirit, everything has a profound effect on me. God shows me the people I meet as He sees them. I view the events of my life from His perspective. I hear the commands of the Lord in his rhythm and obey them."

"Now you're cookin," declared Ben, who sat forward in his chair and put his arms on his knees, interlocking the fingers of both hands. "Are there places I can hear the melody easier than other places? Like, should I have certain times durin the day when I spend quiet time alone with God so I can git in tune?"

"Let me answer that question with a question. If you want to hear classical music live, where do you go?"

"To an orchestra hall, I suppose."

"That's right, and if you want to hear the melody of the Holy Spirit, you go to His orchestra halls. Quiet time with the Lord is one of the venues, but there are others."

"Name some."

"All right. Reading a Bible through the power of the Holy Spirit. Attending a Spirit-filled church – not all are, you know. Playing praise and worship music on long trips in your truck instead of tuning into talk radio. Standing in the serving line of a soup kitchen. Praying here and praying there and praying everywhere. That was Paul's counsel in 1 Thessalonians 5:17."

Ben raised his hand to interrupt me. "How bout thankin God when I'm out plowin my field, or seein His creative powers when I'm deliverin a calf? How about my Friday morning Bible study and spendin time with my children when I'd rather be restin in a chair after a hard day?"

"Those are great places, Ben. And I've felt near to God handing out Bibles to middle-school children. And I've felt near Him when I've held my baby granddaughter."

The third Person who had joined us for coffee – the Holy Spirit – guided us into thoughts beyond our own mental mastery. The three of us spent the rest of the time discussing orchestra halls where the melody of the Holy Spirit plays. There seemed to be no shortage of places.

The radio stations metaphor gave me something I hadn't had before: a measuring stick to show me when I was tuned more into God or more in tune with the world and the inclinations of my natural self. That's what I needed in order to gauge whether I was experiencing more of God most of the time. The Holy Spirit is patient. He spent twenty years bringing me to that point.

MORE OF GOD MOST OF THE TIME

1

Monday, November 21, 2011. My struggle with pancreatic cancer defines my life to such a degree that I can barely remember what I was like before it showed up. Did I once weigh 175 pounds? I can barely remember it. Was there a time I didn't have excruciating pain in my back? It seems like a fantasy. There is no pleasure in a good meal, no restful nights, no carefree walks around the park – only the relentless trudging down a dark road that leads to the graveyard. And, yet, there is hope in Jesus Christ and the gift of eternal life He has promised me. That's what I hang on to.

I'm like the Roman god Janus, with two faces, one looking to the future and one to the past. Ahead, I see the end of my life bearing down on me like an oncoming hearse. Behind, I see the vignettes of my life that led me to experience more of God most of the time. We're told not to dwell on the past, but it's the only safe place for me to live.

Memories fade as time distances us from them. Some experiences, though, are so dramatic they never dim. A person who won the *Reader's Digest Sweepstakes* would never forget the day two people knocked on her door with a camera crew behind them. It was like that with my salvation. I can see the hotel room in my mind, the chair I was sitting in, and the joy in my heart when I accepted Jesus Christ as my Savior. The radio stations metaphor was similar, etched into my memory like deep grooves cut into a metal engraving plate.

My discussion with Ben deepened the grooves, and the radio-stations metaphor became as much a part of me as my hand. God was the leading actor in the drama of my life most of the time; I played the supporting role. It was what I always desired, and now I had it.

Molly came into the office as I was pondering all this and said, "A penny for your thoughts, my darling."

"Make it a dollar, and I will tell you." I mimicked her way of speaking. She never used contractions. She laughed because she knew what I was doing.

"It is a deal."

When I finished telling her what I'd been thinking, she responded with, "I remember your returning from that church service in Northfield ten years ago. I thought you had won the lottery. Excitement was in your eyes and in your voice. It was like the day you came home from Minneapolis and told me you had been saved."

She put her arm around my shoulders and kissed me on the cheek. "How are you doing today?"

"Fine."

"How are you really doing?"

"I try not to think about it. I'm hanging in there. That's all I can do. I'm heading to the office to continue the radio stations metaphor."

✝ ✝ ✝

2003. I wanted to lock the tuning knob of my interior radio station to the exact frequency of the Holy Spirit Station, but it seemed impossible. I'd turn the dial all the way to the right – in my imagination, of course – and hold it there during my hour of prayer and worship. Then it would start to slip back as the demands of the day presented themselves – the phone call I had to make to a client who owed me money, the financial issues I needed to take care of, the dog next door that wouldn't stop barking.

The dial rarely drifted back to a frequency where the World/Self Station was the stronger signal, though sometimes it did. As long as I was in the upper frequencies, there was more of God in my life, and I was in those frequencies most of the time. But as I slipped back from the highest frequencies, I didn't hear the melody of the Holy Spirit as clearly as I wanted.

I tried and tried to keep the dial tuned to 109.7, the highest frequency, until I finally realized it was as vain a dream as pulling all the weeds out of my garden in early May and hoping they wouldn't reappear during the growing season.

It was all I could do to stay above 97.9 – the mid-point – most of the time; and the closer I dropped to that frequency, the more uptight I became. My goal was to remain permanently in the upper frequencies, but I knew I was incapable of doing that without the power of the Holy Spirit. We were a team, with more of Him and less of me. I prayed He would lead me into circumstances and situations where I could hear His station clearly.

One of those situations happened in May 2003 during a visit Molly and I made to Mobile, Alabama to visit the gulf coast. We stopped in Paducah, Kentucky the first night and found a suitable motel off Interstate 24, five miles from downtown. I fell asleep when my head hit the pillow, even with loud semis barreling down the interstate two blocks away. It had been a grueling twelve hours on the road.

Molly did not sleep so well and begged off going with me to see "The Grand Sight" early the next morning. I kept the lights off as she slumbered and slipped quietly out the door, stopping in the front lobby for coffee before heading out to witness first-hand the confluence of the Ohio and Tennessee rivers. I was excited to experience what I'd only read about before in *National Geographic*.

Ten minutes later, with a warm sun settling on my face, I stood on the downtown shore and looked east to the place where the Ohio and Tennessee Rivers came together. It was an impressive sight: the cloudy and churning Ohio River from the north met the lesser Tennessee River coming up from the south. At the point of their confluence, the Tennessee lost its singular identity and took on the name of the Ohio, which flowed westward to empty into the mighty Mississippi.

I walked up and down the shore for the better part of an hour, meditating on the two rivers coming together, and discovered a metaphor in my imagination that brought a spiritual understanding to my mind. I returned to the motel and excitedly related all I had seen and thought to Molly.

"Molly, I went downtown to see the coming together of two rivers and left with a new insight into a deep mystery – how we join together with Christ and flow with Him in this world until we join Him in heaven."

She smiled. "Another one of your metaphors, no doubt?"

"I'd put it in my top five," I answered. "Here's the deal. The greater Ohio River represents the living waters of Jesus Christ as related in the fourth chapter of John. The lesser Tennessee is me before conversion. As the Tennessee takes on the name of the Ohio when they come together, so I took on the name Christian when I joined with Christ in 1982."

"I get your drift, ha ha – pun intended. And then you flow with Christ until you pass into heaven, which is the Mississippi River."

"You've got it. But there's more."

"I am excited to hear the more, but I would be even more excited if you fetched me a cup of coffee from the lobby first." I left and came back with two cups of coffee.

As I handed Molly her coffee, I spoke with unfettered liveliness. "I've often wondered what exactly is in my spirit when once God fills it. The Ohio and Tennessee Rivers flowing as one gives me a clue. The waters of my little river are clear and sterile, flowing without life. The living waters of the Ohio, on the other hand, are mysteriously cloudy and teeming with all God has for me."

"I like where you are going with this and want to give it my undivided attention. I will get ready to leave and we can continue the discussion in the cocoon of our car. We want to make Nashville for lunch." My wife knew I could go on for an hour with one metaphor, walking around it doggedly until I could see all four sides of it.

When we reached the border of Tennessee, I presented my final thought. "Within the deep waters of the Ohio lie the mind, will, and emotions of God. There is Wisdom there, and the mystery of God's presence. When my insignificant self joins with God, He and I become one, with less of me and more of Him."

Molly clapped her hands and looked at me as if I were a prophet of old. "I think that *is* one of your best metaphors."

"Don't think too highly of me, my dear. I didn't come up with the metaphor. The Holy Spirit gave it to me."

"I know that, but I am so blessed to be married to a man to whom the Holy Spirit gives metaphors."

I really didn't like her saying things like that because I struggled with thinking more highly of myself than I should. I was no prophet of old or of the present. I was a servant of God and of the Lord Jesus Christ. I changed the subject.

"I have a question for you. You taught English grammar and punctuation for thirty years at the college. Have you ever in your life ended a sentence with a preposition?" I was referring to her use of *to whom* instead of *a man the Holy Spirit gives metaphors to*.

She put her hand to her mouth and laughed. "I think I did once when I was five years old, and my mother immediately corrected me."

The rest of the trip went smoothly. We enjoyed the trip to Mobile and the surrounding area. I was fascinated with the estuary of Mobile Bay, not knowing the Holy Spirit would unlock the meaning of it two years later in California.

2

Tuesday, November 22, 2011. Today is Molly's birthday. When she came into the bedroom this morning, I put on my best smile and chirped out, "Happy Birthday, my love. Name whatever you want for a present, and I'll give it to you."

She neither returned the smile nor was there joy in her voice. "My only wish is that you will be healed and made whole again." She bent over and kissed me. I had not anticipated that response. I thought she'd say she wanted to visit Joe and Jack for a day, and I was determined to make the trip with her, no matter how bad I felt.

"If I could give you that, my dear, I would. I pray every day for divine healing but hear a whisper within: 'No, My child, no. One day you'll understand.'" Neither of us said anything more.

I have no appetite and force down food because I must. I hate breakfast, despise lunch, and breathe a sigh of relief after finishing supper. I try to drink two malts a day because I can tolerate them better than solid food. I choke down as many supplements as I can; they taste like chalk. My weight is holding at 150 pounds.

I stay as busy as I can writing, or should I say as busy as my health allows. Amidst intense pain and anxiety, somewhere between pleasant memories from the past and dread of the future, I write. It's a struggle. Some days I feel as if I'm 10,000 feet above my body viewing my last thirty years. Some days I feel as if I'm being sucked down a drain.

✝ ✝ ✝

2004. The story of my spiritual life includes many instances of hearing from God. But, rest assured, I was not a hearing-from-God fanatic. Dr. Neil Johnson made sure I didn't stand on street corners or anywhere else telling people I had a word from the Lord. In the summer of 2004, we discussed the matter in depth.

A teacher friend told me the pastor of his church announced to the congregation one Sunday: "The Lord spoke to me and said our church will be one of the top ten houses of deliverance in the United States." Many members didn't feel comfortable with that proclamation, but the majority embraced it. Within a year, the church became a house of carnality, and the pastor had an affair with a fortune teller. I learned from this account that receiving a word from God should be approached with much trepidation, both for the one who hears and for those who hear tell of the revelation. In *Hearing God*, Dallas Willard explains we are given messages that reflect the personality of God in ways we learn to recognize. They are not so much the very words of God but take the form of God's thoughts translated into our thoughts, expressed by us in our own words. In that way we become reflections of Him.

I read Willard's book during July, and it helped me recognize what was probably from the Lord and what was probably not, though such communication is supernatural and cloaked in mystery.

On the second green of our second golf outing of the year, I brought up the topic of hearing from God with Neil, my doctor friend. He dropped his putter and turned to me with exasperation in his voice, "I cringe every time I hear the words 'Thus sayeth the Lord.' Too often the so-called prophets are naïve, deluded, or advancing their own agendas." I remember being taken aback by the fury of his displeasure.

"I don't necessarily disagree with you, Neil, but you don't leave much room for legitimately receiving a message from the Lord." I was standing over a wicked putt when I said that, a steep downhill ten-footer with at least two feet of break. "I've never used the words 'thus sayeth the Lord,' but yet there are times I believe the Lord has spoken to me in exact words."

"Give me an example." Neil picked up his putter. He was still unsettled.

I wasn't in a hurry to putt, hoping the slope would lessen if I didn't think about it. Looking behind to make sure no one was waiting for us to clear the green, I answered Neil. "A few months after we moved to Buffalo, I returned home from a conference I'd attended in Minneapolis, feeling as disconsolate as a man who'd just lost his whole family at sea. I was in a season of deep depression caused by my leaving a job of thirty years and a city I'd lived in for the same amount of time. I sat on a couch in the lower level of our townhome, without hope and with tears in my eyes. 'Jesus have mercy on me,' I cried out over and over, in mental and emotional anguish. It seemed like time stopped, and He answered me with these words: 'Stay out of your mind. I am in your spirit. My presence is all you need.' Calm came over me, and my depression lifted."

Neil said, "Let's continue the conversation after we finish this hole. I'm interested in seeing what you do with your next shot." My putt skidded off the green, and it took two more shots to hole out. Neil also three-putted and we walked in silence to the next hole, which was a par three.

"Good shot," Neil said, as my ball nestled onto the front edge of the green, twenty feet below the pin. Neil's shot was undistinguished.

We drove to a wooded area to escape a passing rain. Neil continued the conversation. "I know you, and I believe you did hear exact words of comfort from Jesus. The big difference between you and the pastor who prophesied his church would become one of deliverance is that yours only related to yourself and is the kind of thing Jesus would say to one in great affliction. I do hope, however, that hearing precise words from God is more an exception for you."

The rain stopped as suddenly as it had started, and we headed down the fairway. I was the cart driver, as I always was for some unknown reason. I have to laugh when I think of what happened next. I turned to look at Neil and hit a big bump that rattled our teeth and tested the strength of our backs. I said, "Ouch. Sorry, Neil. I didn't see that coming." He almost fell out of the cart.

When we returned to a state of physical equilibrium, I continued the discussion. "You are exactly right. I can count on one hand such times. The more common method of hearing from God is when He plants thoughts into my mind that I express with my own words, based on my experiences, education, and personality. It's a daily occurrence. No doubt the same thoughts conveyed into someone else's mind would be expressed in different words." The discussion stopped as we stepped onto the green.

I missed my putt a few inches to the left and tapped in for par. Neil stood over a ten-foot putt with a wicked turn and a steep downhill slope and then backed away. "You know, I don't fully grasp what you're saying any more than I can read the break on this putt." He stroked the ball with trepidation and missed the hole by more than a foot to the left, complaining loudly as the ball went six feet past the hole.

We walked to the next tee box. "Let me put it another way then," I said. "God provides the thoughts and I contribute the words. It's an *us* thing. Dallas Willard confirms this when he explains that God speaks to us with the language of human beings and through the inner sanctum of our own mind. Language is just one of the mediums to express God's thoughts. An artist uses the realm of painting or sculpture to express impressions from the Lord. A musician, her music. Eric Liddle, portrayed in *Chariots of Fire*, said he ran to express God's pleasure."

Neil hit his drive straight down the middle of the fourth fairway and turned to me. "I would say you've just expressed how I hear from the Lord. Can you give me an example of when you thought you were hearing from the Lord but weren't?"

I lost focus trying to think of an example, drove my golf ball into the woods, and threw my driver back into the bag with deadly force. I came out of the trees without finding my ball and dropped another one in the rough and hit a beautiful fade onto the green. I put that club back with respect. "Let me tell you about the time I was driving from Willmar to a college meeting in St. Paul in the spring of 1997, when a prayer entered my mind that I thought was from God.

> Lord, come into my world,
> and show me how to live in it,
> and I'll be a shining light for You.

"If anyone were looking into my car, they'd think I was off my rocker. I grinned from ear to ear and pumped my fist high in the air several times. 'What a wonderful prayer I've just prayed!' Ten seconds later, the Holy Spirit revealed to me it was my prayer without His input. It was a *me* thing. He guided me into an *us* prayer – that is, His enlightenment and my words."

> No! You come into My world,

and I'll show you how to live in it,
and I'll be a shining light for you.

"I didn't have a sense these were the very words of God. It was more a conviction that my first prayer was so far off the mark, it didn't even register as a paltry prayer. When the Holy Spirit turned my thoughts inside-out, I discerned the new words met with God's approval."

Neil hopped out of the cart to hit his second shot and turned to me. "You had me worried with that first self-centered prayer. If God hadn't intervened then, I would have now."

"I know you would have, Neil. But I've told that story to some Christian friends and many of them remarked the first prayer was a wonderful one. My brother Teddy had the same reaction you did."

Neil put both hands on the front of the cart and braced himself as I careened down a steep hill without touching the brake. Neil's face matched the white shirt he was wearing; I think he was praying for safety on the way down. When we reached a level path once more, he hollered at me, "Why do you drive so recklessly?"

"I don't know. Someone has to."

"That doesn't make any sense," Neil said, still with a loud voice.

"I know it doesn't. It's not meant to make sense. I'm just a mischievous Paul who does unexplainable things by instinct. Sorry if it alarmed you." I really didn't know why I did such things. It's almost as if the prankster from my youth popped up every now and again and exerted his will.

"Where were we?" said Neil, still perplexed by my uninhibited antics. "Oh yes, I think some people pray mechanically without giving much thought to what they say. I can't count the number of times I've heard the prayer, 'Jesus be with me in my troubles,' or whatever the issue is. I generally don't say anything, but sometimes mention that Jesus is always with them if they're Christians. More to the point is whether they're with Him."

The hole we were playing was a par five, and Neil stepped out of the cart to hit his third shot to the green. By this time, he had lost his concentration and hit an eight iron so miserably that he walked to his ball without getting back into the cart. I remember laughing at his ineptitude and his scowling back at me.

The word *most* leaves room for something else. If most fruits and vegetables are good to eat, there must be some that aren't. My listening to the Holy Spirit Station most of the time left room to listen to the World/Self Station some of the time. Although I was saved from sin, I still missed the mark too often, in my opinion. Impatience was my greatest fault.

3

Tuesday, November 29, 2011. Molly is anxious about my loss of weight and loss of energy. She came into the office this morning and put her left arm around my shoulder, as she often did, and whispered into my right ear. "I think we should call your doctor and ask if he can do something. You are wasting away."

"I'm afraid there's less of me for you to love every day."

"How can you say such a thing? This is serious."

"It's called gallows humor. If I took everything seriously, I'd be camped out on the doorstep of a psychiatrist from morning to night. Go ahead and call the doctor."

"Maybe a feeding tube would give you the nourishment you need," she suggested.

I perked up. "Hey, let's ask him about a feeding tube. I shudder every time I even think about eating."

She set up a conference call with Dr. DeAngelo. "It's too early for a feeding tube," he said. "Besides, it's uncomfortable and can have unpleasant side-effects."

When he said "unpleasant side effects," I thought of the misadventure with chemotherapy and said, "That's the end of talking about a feeding tube." To me now, quality of life is more important than quantity of life. I don't want to take chances with additional problems; I will have enough complications without adding something I don't need to.

Molly asked, "Is there anything else that would help?"

Dr. DeAngelo's voice started to crack. I could imagine him sitting behind his desk trying to control his emotions. To him, I was not just another patient. I was like family.

"I'll set up an appointment with a nutritionist I know. She's worked with other patients of mine and will show you the easiest foods to eat and high-nutrition liquids to drink. I'll also send a prescription to your pharmacy for a medication that could help your appetite, as well as any depression you might have."

Any depression I might have? Who wouldn't be depressed with a death sentence? But it wasn't a deep depression. The Lord has kept me from falling into a bottomless pit.

When we turned off the cell phone, Molly felt crushed. "I am sorry, darling. I thought a feeding tube might be a good solution for your weight loss." Her head hung low.

"Come over here, Molly," I said and lifted up her head so I could look her straight in the eyes. "I know you love me and want whatever is best for me. This was something to explore. I thought it was a good idea. The fact of the matter is I feel better knowing a nutritionist and medication will help." I kissed her full on the lips and we held onto each other for nearly ten minutes, without saying a word. My condition would be unbearable without her love, without her compassionate care. She gives strength to this sickly body.

We moved to the sun room and talked for an hour about the things that were important to us, the most important one being the relationship not only between us but also with our Savior and the Lord of our lives. Without Him, there is no meaning to any of it.

✝ ✝ ✝

2005. In the spring of this year, the Holy Spirit apparently felt it was time to reinforce the interior radio station vision because I had a "doing it my way" disposition with a particular situation. Adam and Eve "did it their way" and bequeathed that to all of us. My way or His way was a struggle that never ended.

A Christian magazine had commissioned me to write an article that covered the interaction between spirit and soul in the life of a believer. To explain the interactions with logic would have been easy; but this was to be a practical commentary, not a theological dissertation. I needed a metaphor and was impatient because I couldn't think of a good one.

I called my brother Teddy and asked him for a metaphor. "How about the yoke and white of an egg intermixing?" he offered. "The yolk is the spirit and the white is the soul."

"You don't think I've already come up with that?" I said with an unbrotherly tone of voice. "Once the yolk and white mix together, they can't be unmixed; and that's not the way the Christian life works. It's not one mixing and we're done. There's an ongoing ebb and flow of spirit and soul."

"Not every metaphor is a perfect explanation," Teddy responded with a defensive undertone. "You're too much of a perfectionist, Paul. You were that way growing up and you still are."

"That's not fair, Teddy. I *was* a perfectionist growing up but you of all people should know how hard I've worked to diminish its control over me."

His voice softened. "I do know you're not the Paul I grew up with, but your wanting everything to be done just right for so many years has left a scar in me. When we were kids, my piano playing was never up to your standards. When we were teenagers, you kept pointing out the errors in my golf swing even though I beat you most of the time. Your comment that my metaphor was not good enough brought me back to the old days. Sorry."

"And I'm sorry for reverting back to my critical days. Let's change subjects. How's your counseling practice doing?"

I called Martin next, and the best he could do was the overlapping of two circles, one being the spirit and the other the soul. I'd seen that one before; it was too static. Ben and Bruce came up with examples that were too mundane to even mention.

I was edgy and peevish before we left for California. I wanted to send the article off before leaving. The deadline was ten days away.

Molly tried to be helpful. "Maybe you are trying too hard, darling. The trip to your sister's may be a good time to relax and see what the Holy Spirit has in mind."

"If He had something in mind, He should've given it to me by now." How could I have been that unkind and rude? The impatient part of me was firmly in control.

Molly shook her head and said no more. We left the next day for a March visit to my sister's home in Palm Desert, California to escape the cold still gripping Minnesota.

Katrina, my sister, and Santiago, her husband, met us at the Palm Springs airport. The temperature was in the 70s and 80s for our whole trip, with hardly a cloud in the sky. It should have been a carefree time, but I was troubled by my lack of an illustration to explain the mixing of soul and spirit in the life of a believer.

Molly went for long walks with Katrina, and Santiago practiced medicine at two different clinics, so I had plenty of time to meditate on metaphors on the back veranda and on solitary walks. But I might just as well have been trying to figure out the Trinity. My restlessness of soul didn't have me shaking my fist at God in a huff, but I was heading in that direction. On the day before we returned to Minnesota, I was about to pull my beard out. The deadline was three days away.

I made a final hike into the foothills surrounding Palm Desert and sat down on a large rock shaped like a table. With discouragement and frustration, I cried out, "I give up. I can't figure this out." It's not that I hadn't prayed for insight from the Holy Spirit, but those prayers were of a "help-me-figure-it-out" type. I see now the Holy Spirit was waiting for an "I-give-up" prayer.

A blazing sun was baking everything in the desert; the rock I sat on blistered my behind. Unexpectedly, for the sky had been clear, a cloud flittered across the sun and a cool breeze came down from the mountains. A memory from long ago floated into my mind.

It was the trip Molly and I had taken to tour the Alabama and Northwest Florida Gulf shore. We had spent a full day rummaging around Mobile Bay. Sitting on that rock in the mountain foothills of Coachella Valley, my imagination showed me the waves of the bay gently lapping the shore, with seagulls everywhere.

The distinctive ocean smell filled my nostrils, and I saw myself studying a geographic marker with the diligence of a lawyer examining a legal contract. Molly was standing across the street watching helplessly as the minutes ticked by. I shouted to her, "Mobile Bay is the fourth largest estuary in the United States." I could see her put her hand to her mouth to signify a yawn. The mixture of fresh water and salt water in the estuary fascinated me, but I didn't think any deeper about it than a general appreciation. It didn't take long for the experience to become lost in the dustbin of my subconscious after a few weeks.

But here it was again, present in my consciousness in full color. With that flashback, the Holy Spirit gave me the metaphor I was searching for. I leaped off the rock and ran home to my sister's place. Molly and Katrina were back from their walk and talking on the veranda, enjoying the now cloudy weather and cool breeze.

I typed "what is an estuary?" into the search box of Santiago's computer: "An estuary is when a coastal body of fresh water has an open connection with a body of salt water, such as the Mobile, Tensaw, and a few other rivers emptying into the northern reaches of Mobile Bay." I grabbed my notepad and wrote furiously, through the power of the Holy Spirit.

The salt water represents my soul and the fresh water the Holy Spirit. An estuary is the place where the waters meet. The northern half has a higher concentration of fresh water; translated, more of the Holy Spirit. The southern half has more salt water; that is, more of the world and my natural self. When I'm dwelling in the northern part of the estuary, I'm immersed in the Holy Spirit. In the southern region, I'm soaking in the world and my own inclinations.

This metaphor isn't a perfect representation – none of them are – but it's as close as I can come to the divine mystery of the mixing of soul and spirit because it's a fluid representation. I'm not in one place or another all the time. In my morning prayer time, I'm far up in the northern waters. Two hours later I may be in the southern waters after the stock market drops 300 points, then in the afternoon make my way into the northern waters again when I visit a guy named Marv, who's dying of muscular dystrophy.

I've been in the southern waters with my frustration and impatience for the past few weeks. But the Holy Spirit has breathed into the sails of my little boat and propelled me in a direct line north, where dwells His presence and influence in my life. I was too long absent.

What amazing work the Holy Spirit performed. He gave me an effective illustration of the mixing of spirit and soul and convicted me of living away from Him at the same time. The Mobile Bay metaphor had dynamics similar to the interior radio band one. The northern waters were like the higher frequencies and the southern waters like the lower frequencies.

I believe the Holy Spirit doubled down to make me aware in two different but similar contexts how closely I'm in tune with Him at any given time and how diligently I'm following Jesus Christ. I need only ask Him to show me where I am on the radio band or what hemisphere of the estuary I'm living in – and He shows me time after time after time.

I called Teddy at once on my cell phone.

4

Wednesday, November 30, 2011. Molly and I met at just the right time, not too early and not too late. She was single and so was I. We were both content with our unmarriedness, being equally independent and carefree. She didn't need a husband; I didn't need a wife. We were both new hires at the college in Willmar.

I knew she was single from Friday afternoon faculty socials at a local tavern marking the end of the week. She was a Christian who didn't drink alcohol. I wasn't a Christian then, though I thought I was, and enjoyed having a couple of beers.

I found myself sitting at her table each Friday, and we became acquainted. She was a former Homecoming Queen and Miss Ellendale, was thoughtful and quiet, and had a good sense of humor. After a month of Fridays, I thought to myself, "Now here is a girl I could marry." Such a thought had never appeared in my soul before. She admitted later to having the same thoughts. But I didn't have the courage to ask her for a date. What if she turned me down? I didn't want to take the chance.

One day in late September, we met in a hallway near the college bookstore. She asked if I was going to watch the Vikings football game that Sunday. I told her I couldn't because the cabin I was renting didn't have cable TV; the only station available played polka music on Sundays. I almost fell to the floor when she invited me over to her apartment to watch the game. Then she sealed the deal by fixing supper for the two of us.

After that, I was a regular visitor to her place on Sundays. The food connection carried over to school: we had lunch together in the cafeteria every noon. And we spent many hours a week together outside of school. I visited her hometown and met her parents. She did the same with my parents. I was love-struck and felt incomplete when she was not around. She suffered from the same affliction. We married the next summer.

Molly was the best thing that ever happened to me, other than my salvation, which came a few years after we were married. When our two boys were born, our love deepened. I can't imagine what my life would have been like without the three of them. As the boys grew up, I became involved in all their sports, volunteering to be a coach, following them around on traveling teams, and chasing them around the Upper Midwest during their college careers. Our relationship is still wonderfully strong today. Too soon it will end.

My life is full of lasts. Today is the last day of November; I'll never see another. The yellowness of my skin is becoming more pronounced and the whites of my eyes glow like the flames in my fireplace. My next doctor's appointment is in less than two weeks. I'll ask him what can be done. Molly is bothered by it, as are my friends, though none of them say anything. I expect they see it as I do – "the mask of death."

✝ ✝ ✝

2005. Back to the phone call with Teddy from California that March. "Well, Teddy, what do you say? What do you think of the metaphor the Holy Spirit gave me?"

Teddy waited a few seconds to tease me, a trait that carried over from the time we were kids and I was the younger brother. "I would say that, in my humble opinion, with all due respect to the time you have spent searching for an answer, that…" Teddy paused for effect.

"For heaven's sake, just spit it out! Tell me what you think!" I was exasperated, just like I'd been when I was nine-years old waiting for Teddy to tell me whether we were going out in the backyard to play catch or head to Ronnie's house to play Monopoly.

"Well," said Teddy, with the playfulness he enjoyed in stringing me along, "I'd say you nailed it. You've absolutely nailed it." I started writing the article as soon as we hung up and created a rough draft in three hours.

There was one other person I wanted to share the metaphor with before writing the final manuscript – my spiritual partner Ben. I called him from California and set up a meeting at the coffee shop for the morning after we returned. That would still give me a day to make refinements and send it off, though I was uncomfortable with rubbing up so closely to the deadline. It was not my style.

Bennett Macdonald and I, though fast friends and brothers-in-Christ, had few natural commonalities. I grew up in a town of 6,000 souls; Ben was a farm lad who became the owner of 800 acres when his father died at a young age. I was well educated, having graduated from a four-year college and in possession of two graduate degrees. Ben had a high-school diploma and a two-year community college degree in agriculture. He also had a doctor's degree in common sense and spiritual discernment.

It was that time of year in Minnesota that was not quite winter and not quite spring. Snow had fallen the night before and turned to slush with the rising morning temperatures. Mother Nature couldn't make up her mind which she wanted to be. In other words, it was mid-March in Minnesota. The floor of the coffee shop was wet and slippery.

I was first to arrive and trotted over to the two leather chairs in front of the fireplace. I should have known better than to walk so fast. My feet went out from underneath me, and my arms flopped helplessly in the air, as if they were searching for a handle to keep me from falling to the floor. My neck and back were about to need three chiropractors to put me back together. I yelled, "Oh, no!" on the way down but didn't hit the floor. A heavy-set man, whom I had often seen but never talked to, jumped out of his chair with a speed I would not have thought possible for someone so corpulent… and caught me.

"How can I ever thank you?" I said, while steadying myself.

"At your service," he replied. "We go to the same church." I'd never seen him there.

I sat in one of the two leather chairs, still shaking from my near disaster. Five minutes later, Ben came in dressed like a lumberjack from the forests of northern Minnesota. He had taken a break from splitting wood outside his barn and would be going back to complete the job when we were done. Ben was what you'd call a practical Christian. "If Holy Spirit insights can't be put into practice, they're like scraps of paper blowin in the wind," he often said.

I told him about my near fall. He answered with, "God watchin over you again. He must get paid overtime."

"I'm sure He does." I know He does. From the time I was born with yellow jaundice and expected to die, He has protected me. "Let me tell you why I wanted to meet with you right away," and enthusiastically related the metaphor, rubbing my hands together at the end as if to say, "How do you like that?"

Ben stared at me with a deadpan face and asked in his droll way, "I kinda get what you're talkin about, but how does it play out in real life?"

My pride instantly departed. "He wants a story. Holy Spirit, show me something in my life that puts insight into action."

My coffee was cold, so I went to the counter for a refill. Fortunately there was a lengthy line to allow me to recollect a story from the past. I returned to the table and announced, "I'm ready."

"Ready for what?" Ben replied.

"Ready to tell you how the estuary metaphor works in real life. Isn't that what you wanted?"

Ben smiled and nodded and leaned back in what he called "my listening position" as I related the following story.

"As you know, I used to be president of our townhome association and one year had a most unpleasant experience. On Christmas morning, a member of our association came pounding on my door. Our service provider was plowing snow from a heavy storm, and Darl complained to me that they should have plowed his driveway first because he was expecting company. I'd had trouble with him before and my response was not kind. He left like a man who'd just been punched in the gut and said, 'You'll regret this.'

"It wasn't but ten minutes later when an email from him scorched my computer. I could have let that bounce off me, knowing what a curmudgeon he was, but he copied the email to everyone else in the association, making me out to be a heartless and mean-spirited wretch. I was not about to let him get by with his accusations and sent him a return email that made his seem like a compliment, copying it also to all members of the association. So started an on-line battle in which there could be no winner, and neither one of us was about to call a truce.

"The battle went on for nearly a week and preoccupied my mind, will, and emotions for the better part of each day. I can't believe I was so caught up in it. I had not wandered aimlessly away from the spiritual path I was walking. I had leaped headfirst from it and landed in a ditch, from where I couldn't observe how damaging my behavior was. I'm ashamed now just telling you about it."

"You should be. I woulda never thought you capable of somethin that revengeful. I'm sorry; I shouldn't be so cruel in my response. It's just that...."

I interrupted Ben. "No, you're right on. It was like two pigs wallowing in the mud. I can't believe I was so oblivious to my conduct. Molly told me to stop sending those awful emails, but I cut her off short. 'I need to defend myself from that reprobate,' I remember telling her. 'If I don't who will?' Referring to the Estuary of Mobile Bay metaphor, I was anchored in the far southern regions, filled with the salt water of my own selfish self and blind to the Holy Spirit trying to catch my attention.

"But catch my attention He did, since I'd asked Him many times before to convict me when I wandered far enough from God that I couldn't feel His presence. I had slammed shut the door to my soul but hadn't latched it. Five days after the war commenced, the Holy Spirit opened the door and threw some light into my soul. He showed me how my thoughts and actions saddened my Father. I imagined His face wet with tears when He saw His child caught up in nastiness and revenge. How far I had fallen from following His Son! I wept. And then the Holy Spirit did something I hadn't been able to do on my own, and might not have done in my self-righteous anger. He opened the sails of my little boat to His influence and pushed me back up into the northern reaches of Mobile Bay, where there was more of God than me.

"My whole attitude changed. I repented of my rebelliousness and prayed for a way to end the battle. Unconcerned whether I won or not, ready in fact to lose. As I escaped my natural self in weighty prayer, one thing became clear: stop sending emails no matter what he does. It seems so obvious now and shouldn't have taken five days to realize. Being caught up in revenge is like building a wall so high you can't see over it.

"Jesus said to pray for our enemies, so I swallowed my pride and prayed for the guy. That was as difficult as praying for a man who'd just hit me in the face. Harmony returned to the neighborhood, and it seemed my prayers for the fellow had an effect: he became less openly negative and critical.

"Well, Ben, does that help you see what the estuary metaphor looks like in real life?" Ben grinned in a way only he could. It was somewhere between a smirk and a smile.

"Yup, Paul, sure I understand it now."

I left the coffee shop and raced home to put the final touches to the magazine article, including the story I had just related to Ben. I sent it out in the afternoon, one day before it was due. I thought that ended the discussion of the estuary metaphor with Ben, but he brought it up at our next coffee.

5

Wednesday, December 7, 2011. Fatigue envelops me like a shroud. I have accepted that divine healing is not the outcome reserved for me and great suffering will follow me to the grave. But He has said He will be with me to the end, and I believe that with all my heart. I pray only for a clear mind to complete my narrative, especially with the morphine I'm taking.

Last Thursday the pain in my back was so intense I couldn't get out of bed. My contorted face drove Molly to tears. "I'm calling the ambulance," she said with a voice of desperation.

I forced my voice out through gasps and wheezes. "Not yet, my dear; I may get better later on." I shuddered at the thought of riding in an ambulance over bumpy roads.

"I am not waiting for later on. You are going to the ER now!"

The pain lessened just enough so I could joke. "That's being rather pushy, isn't it?"

She tried not to look amused but couldn't help herself. "You must be feeling better. I am glad," she said while stifling a giggle.

"I know it's a serious business, but if I can't bring humor into it, we'd both be in the bottom of a mine shaft."

My respite from extreme pain ended quickly, and I screamed out to Molly, "Please call the ambulance as soon as you can!"

She picked up the phone and five minutes later an ambulance whisked me away to the emergency room. Dr. DeAngelo arrived ten minutes after we did. He boosted the morphine, which took me by the hand into a never-never land, where I drifted in and out of a peaceful fog for several days.

I'm able to write this morning. The pain is more bearable, and the mental fog has lifted.

✞ ✞ ✞

2005. My story continues with Ben in the same coffee shop seven days later. The weather had turned unseasonably warm, more like May than March. The water and mud from last week were long gone. We both arrived in the parking lot at the same time and walked to the coffee shop with an enthusiastic sun awakening our bodies and our souls. It was a good day to be alive. I entered the front door first and saw two people already sitting in the leather chairs in front of the fireplace. I turned around and told Ben, "Why don't you go over and tell them their time is up?"

Ben laughed. "Why don't you tell them yourself? You're the first one in; it's your responsibility."

We threw our notepads on a table in the general area and proceeded to the counter. I ordered a latte instead of my usual coffee.

"What's up with the latte?" Ben asked.

"I'm celebrating the arrival of spring."

"Well, then, I'll have a latte too."

I headed back to the table first and was about to sit down when the two people in our leather chairs got up to leave. With a nimbleness that amused the other patrons, I grabbed Ben's notebook and tossed it on one of the chairs before the young husband and wife took a step. Then I jumped into the other chair from the side to avoid hitting the lady, who turned around when she heard the sound of a body hitting leather and laughed. When Ben arrived he was pleasantly surprised. "Well, did you tell them they hada leave?"

"I did, but they weren't going to give up their places until I told them you were my enforcer and would throw them out the front door. They looked at your size, jumped up in alarm, and left."

"Yah, sure, I bet they laughed so hard they could hardly breathe and giggled all the way to the door." Ben's face took on a serious look; he didn't continue the joke or engage in chit-chat. In fact he stopped talking. I figured he had an agenda item up for discussion but didn't want to advance it in case I had one. He always deferred to me. It was a trait of his selfless character.

"You're thinking about something, Ben. What is it?" That was his opening, and he took it.

"I been thinkin about the Mobile Bay Estuary and what you said bout bein nearer God in the northern part and farther from Him in the southern part. Can you stretch that out a bit?"

"With pleasure, my friend, but first I need to fetch my Bible from the car." The weather was so nice I walked in slow motion to absorb the fresh air.

When I sat back down, I said, "I've also been thinking and praying since our last discussion." I took a sip of my latte and watched people coming into the coffee shop in short sleeve shirts. A few wore shorts. "All metaphors break down somewhere, and Mobile Bay is no exception. The Holy Spirit is a Person, not a body of water or an electrical force or anything else we humans use to explain Him." I opened my Bible to John 17, read verses 20-26, and tapped my right forefinger on the passage three times with enough force that it could have been called a thumping, which caught Ben's attention.

"This is a great mystery, Ben, that we are in Jesus in the same way Jesus describes his relationship with His Father: 'just as you are in me and I am in you. May they also be in us.' I understand in the abstract what Jesus means, but I'm a visual guy and need an illustration. That's why the metaphor of an estuary makes sense to me. It doesn't give me the entire reality of our relationship with God, but it gives a glimpse.

"Let me read a verse that speaks plainly." I turned to James 4:8. "Come near to God and he will come near to you." I punctuated the page again with three thumps. "I am either nearer God or farther away, and everything in-between. And the closeness starts with me."

Ben had that same trademark look of a sly smile. "I kinda get what you're talkin about, but how does it play out in real life?" This time I was ready with a story.

"Back in my college-administrator days, I had a colleague who 'wears her religion on her sleeve,' as the president of the college remarked to me once. And she did. She once told me a story of a time she was heading to a revival meeting one-hundred miles from her house and stopped on the shoulder of a highway after going twenty miles. It had entered her mind that she should have stayed home to care for a sick friend. She prayed for twenty minutes, with the wind from big trucks rattling her car. The Lord led her to proceed ahead; but before she did, she called her friend back home who said she was doing much better. I could tell you many stories of how she lived out her

Christianity. She was one I would say lived in close proximity to Jesus – most of the time.

"But there were a few occasions when she fell back into the natural world. I'll never forget an administrative meeting when the college president took her to task for not following one of his directives. I was afraid of what might happen next when I saw her face turn red and heard her shallow breathing. She stood up and glared at the president for several seconds, as if she were about to shoot him. Then, unable to control herself, she swore at him with R-rated words and stormed out of the conference room, slamming the door shut so furiously it seemed to vibrate for a few seconds. I was aghast, as we all were. She apologized for her behavior at the next cabinet meeting, but the damage had been done. A year later, the president had an opportunity to get rid of her and he did. But God didn't get rid of her. Joyce soon found a different job within the state-college system more suitable for her.

"Here's an illustration from the opposite direction. During summers in Willmar, I played golf nearly every Sunday after church with a member of my Friday-morning Bible study. He often brought along a member of his church named Les, who was the exact opposite of Joyce. Les used course language, boasted about taking advantage of people in his business dealings, and talked about women as if they were commodities. In fact, Les was taken to court for sexual harassment about three years before I started playing with him. Rumor was he paid off a key witness not to testify and was acquitted.

"I stayed away from Les as much as was possible in a group that moved together as a unit, though he sometimes sought me out to tell me how he'd screwed someone over or made a ton of money in a shady business venture. His arrogance was an affront to my sensibilities.

"One Sunday when the sun was bright and the wind only a mild breeze, he was unusually quiet and thoughtful. I hadn't seen that Les before. As we walked off the ninth green, he announced he wouldn't be playing the back side with us. He said the Holy Spirit had impressed upon him to visit a lonely member of the church in a nursing home, a man with depression who needed encouragement to make it through each day, especially Sundays. So much for generalizations."

Ben's face looked like a question mark. "I enjoyed both stories, Paul, but didn't exactly catch the meanin. I can tell you stories bout

Jekyll and Hyde people I know, but isn't that kinda the way the world is?"

"It *is* the way the world is, Ben, unfortunately. Let me explain why I told you those anecdotes. We've discussed before that many Christians are a flighty lot, changing their spiritual colors like chameleons. Joyce was supposedly a model Christian, but she had an earthy side that was not becoming. And Les was an earthy Christian who had a more spiritual side every now and again."

"How do you know Les was a Christian?" Ben asked. "He sure doesn't sound like one."

"I guess I don't know for certain. I once asked my Bible-study friend the same question, and he told me of discussions he'd had with Les and things he'd seen that led him to believe he was a Christian. But only God knows in the end."

Ben studied me with a look somewhere between Stephen when he was about to be stoned and Francis of Assisi looking at the birds. "Let me tell you what I'm thinkin bout this, and you let me know if I'm on target or not."

"All right. I'm listening."

"I'd say most Christians have times they're walkin right alongside Jesus and times they're laggin a few miles behind, payin more attention to the world than to Him. And I'd say the Holy Spirit lives in us to teach us about Jesus and push us to stay near Him. I know there are times I'm prayin with my family at breakfast and swearin at my tractor an hour later. I'm like one of them chameleons you was talking about. The Holy Spirit is always with me, but I'm not always with Him."

I looked at the fireplace with its tongue-like flames and then at Ben, who'd just explained being near or far from God in five sentences much better than I had in five paragraphs.

6

Friday, December 9, 2011. Ben came over to visit me yesterday afternoon. I was lying on the couch in the living room when he knocked; Molly was out shopping. I shuffled to the front door, let him in, and steered him to the kitchen table.

"I miss our coffee times," he said.

"So do I. Do you want to have a cup of coffee with me and pretend we're at our regular spot?"

"Sure. Do you want me to get it?"

"No, I don't want to give up my independence quite yet."

With coffee in hand and an awkward silence before us, Ben asked, "How are you doing?"

"Fine," I answered.

"How are you *really* doing?" Other than Molly, he's the only one who has asked me for the truth. His second question moved us beyond chit-chat.

"If I told you how I really felt, you'd never come visit again."

"That's not true; I would." But he wouldn't. The truth of my condition would take a half hour to relate and would stand his hair on end. He'd be so uncomfortable he'd be counting the minutes until he could safely leave, worried I might die on his watch. And when I'd completed my tale of woe, I'd be worried I might pass away right in front of him.

I didn't want to go down that path so changed the subject on him. "How are things going on the farm?" That question elicited a thirty-minute monolog, which was what I wanted. Speaking expends too much energy; I'd much rather listen.

When Ben left, I dragged myself down the hallway to write the next chapter. My mind is still sharp, but my body is a disaster.

✝ ✝ ✝

2006. In November, my brother Teddy made one of his random phone calls. "What's up bro? I haven't talked to you for three weeks."

"Not much." That was my default answer to give myself time to think. Actually, quite a bit had happened in the past three weeks, and I pulled out my highlights journal to prepare myself for his next question.

"Not much? For a guy who's walking with the Lord more than anyone I know, other than myself of course, how can you say, 'Not much'?"

"I admire your humility, Teddy. It's so becoming on you." We both laughed. "Actually, something very important did happen to me since we last talked. It was a God thing."

"I'm all ears."

"You remember I was going to the Gettysburg Battlefield by myself two days after we last talked."

"I do indeed. Molly didn't want to go and trail along as you examined every last cannon on the site."

"I have to confess that I missed two cannons on the Cemetery Ridge side."

"Tell me about the trip! I'm on pins and needles waiting to hear it."

"Yeah, yeah. I can just see you on pins and needles."

"You've got me there, Paul. Actually I'm sitting in a lounge chair with my feet up, looking out the patio window at the nature pond north of my backyard." I'd been at Teddy's new house in North Carolina in the past year and had a picture in my mind of where he was.

I glanced at the account of my Gettysburg Adventure in my highlights journal so I wouldn't leave anything out. "It was an adventure of a lifetime – but didn't start well. Molly dropped me off in the departure area of the Minneapolis airport. I walked to the check-in counter and reached into my pocket for my driver's license, but the pocket was empty. I had forgotten my wallet at home in Buffalo. Panic overtook me. It would take Molly two-and-a-half hours at best to make the round trip to Buffalo and back, and the plane was due to take off in an hour and twenty minutes.

"I was paralyzed and full of myself – *my* trip, *my* plane, *my* loss – and the gates of my soul that let in the Holy Spirit slammed shut. I immediately knew what had happened because of the two metaphors given to me in the past. They were front and center in my mind to inform me of whether I was in tune with the Holy Spirit and to what degree.

"My interior radio dial showed that I was in the lower frequencies, closer to the World/Self station than the Holy Spirit station. And I could see that I was in the southern hemisphere of the Mobile Bay estuary.

"I prayed with abandon: 'Holy Spirit, take over my mind, will, and emotions. I want to make this trip; and if that's in God's will for me, it will somehow happen. But if the trip doesn't work out, that will be OK as well.' I felt a wonderful peace as I put everything in God's hands. He was officially in charge.

"I asked the person at the ticket counter if there was a later flight. She said, 'We have a flight one hour from your scheduled one, and there's a seat open, but you will incur an extra $350 charge.' Before I could say a word, she smiled reassuringly: 'I'll waive the extra charge.'

"My new flight would leave the gate in two hours and twenty minutes, not enough time for Molly to make the roundtrip and for me to make it through security. Even so, I felt supernaturally at peace. Somehow it was going to work out, not because of anything I could do but because He was in charge. An hour later I checked the departure time, and it changed before my eyes to be fifteen minutes late. Then the miraculous happened: Molly made the trip to Buffalo and back in two hours and ten minutes. She said every light was green and the traffic was uncharacteristically light for that time of day. I was on board with a few minutes to spare.

"And that's the way the whole trip went. More of God and less of me. Instead of planning everything out as I usually did, I left myself open to His plans. When I needed information, the right person showed up. When I lost my smartphone at an airport candy counter in St. Louis on my way back to Minneapolis, it was returned to me in a most unusual way. Every morning when I arose in Gettysburg, I spent time in prayer asking the Holy Spirit for His guidance for that day, and everything fell into place. In a way, it was as if I'd lost my life to my own will and found it again in His."

"Great story, Paul."

Since we hadn't connected for almost a month, our phone conversation continued beyond the usual half hour. I could envision Teddy hunkered down in his lounge chair gazing into the backyard. It's where he sat when we had some long discussions the week Molly and I were at his place.

7

Saturday, December 10, 2011. Pancreatic cancer is like a black box. I entered it on October 14, 2011 and will exit it when God sees fit, I think not long from now. Within the box, I have no control over what's physically happening to me. I do however have control over my mind, will, and emotions.

When I woke up this morning, the first thing I saw was Molly, dozing peacefully in the chair near the bed. I watched her until she awoke. No worried look was on her face, no frowns, and no tears. A slight smile indicated she might be having a pleasant dream.

Slowly her eyes opened, and she looked at me looking at her. "How long have you been watching me?" she asked softly.

"About thirty minutes."

"You should have gotten me up. Do you need anything?"

"I've already obtained everything I need." Her face became a question mark.

"My one need was to see you free of all worries about me. Your expression was like the first time I woke up alongside you after our wedding – perfectly content and brimming with joy."

Molly blushed. "I will never forget that morning. There was a man in my bed looking at me when I opened my eyes. 'What have I done?' was my first thought. Then when you tenderly kissed me, I knew I had made the best decision of my life. I have never regretted one minute of our life together."

"Neither have I."

I am thankful for friends who provide respite care for Molly so she can have time for herself. Being my nurse, caretaker, cook, and physical therapist is too much responsibility to continue non-stop. The almost total dependence I have on others now is a stark contrast to the independence I cherished before I met Molly. Perhaps God is using this as an exclamation mark to my unconditional dependence on Him.

Though it's a Saturday, something tells me I should write one chapter this morning before something ominous happens, I know not what.

✞ ✞ ✞

2006. Continuing on with the November phone conversation with Teddy. My Gettysburg story had reached its conclusion; and it was my turn to listen to Teddy relate a story about dying to his natural self, which was much like mine. I laid my cell phone on the computer table, on speaker mode, and walked around my home office as I listened to him. I stared out the north-side window and watched a soft November rain giving a last drink of water to our auburn brown front lawn before winter set in. His story was about a trip to Romania to serve as a resource to Christian pastors. He finished it with, "It was impossible for me to accomplish the awesome things that happened; but with God, all things are possible."

"They are, of a certainty," I acknowledged. I turned around to speak into the reclining phone. "It's time to bring my favorite Christian author into the conversation, Teddy."

"I expect that would be C.S. Lewis," declared Teddy.

"Of course. Who else?" C.S. Lewis was a favorite author for both of us, but more so for me. In the bookcase against the west wall of my office, there resided a collection of every book Lewis ever wrote, a number of biographies written about him, and several compilations by subject matter. They took up four feet on two shelves.

"Could you take your phone off speaker mode so I can hear you better. You're starting to crack up."

That was his way of saying, "I'm hard of hearing and need your lips near the phone, and talk to me as if we're together in person and I'm twenty feet away."

"OK," I yelled, at the volume of a man shouting 'fire' in a crowded theater. "Can you hear me now?"

"Egad! You don't have to scream at me."

"Is this better?" I said in a voice I used with my mother in her last years.

"Yes, much better. Thank you."

119

"What were we talking about?" I asked, knowing full well what we were talking about.

"C.S. Lewis and dying to self."

"Right. Owen Barfield was a close friend of Lewis' for 44 years and made this observation about him: 'At a certain stage of his life, he deliberately ceased to take any interest in himself.'"

"Did you just pull out a book from one of the tall bookcases in your office to find that?"

"No, it's permanently in the library of my mind. However, I did pull out Lewis' work called *The Weight of Glory* and found the part where he refers to the words of John the Baptist in John 3:30 – 'He must become greater; I must become less.'

"I wrote these words in the margin, paraphrasing what Lewis had to say about that verse: 'God is not looking for a partial surrender of our lives, not a bit of a compromise, but as He gives Himself totally to us, we are to give ourselves totally to Him… nothing less.'

"Lewis concludes his thought with this phrase: 'only in so far as our self-affirming will retires and makes room for Him in our souls.'"

"Hmm," said Teddy, "he was one wise Christian. Now I'm going to take a page out of your friend Ben's book. How does forgetting about yourself play out in your own life?"

"An appropriate question. Let me think." There was a pause of a minute, not an unusual happening with us. I broke the silence with a story that crept into my mind from a file cabinet in the back row of my memory. "How about this? My family changed churches in Willmar some twenty years ago because the one we were attending was moving away from Biblical principles. You remember the story."

"I do indeed. You asked me if you should stay in that church and try to be an agent for change or go elsewhere. I told you a church was a hard thing to move once it was going the wrong way, especially if the pastor and enough of the congregation were following a path of apostasy."

"It was that advice," I replied, "that led me to find another church. The pastor and all the elders were angry with me for leaving and dragging my family along. A month after we left, a woman in the Bible study I'd been a member of called me. Her name was Ruby.

"She asked if I'd be willing to teach the ten o'clock Sunday school class I belonged to for four years. The leader of that class, a sweet little old lady named Peggy, had recently died.

"I wanted to say, 'Are you out of your mind? Everyone hates me back there. How could I come back to lead a Bible study?' Instead, I politely said, 'I don't think that would be a good idea, Ruby.'

"What followed was a long week of grappling with God. I told Him it would be crazy for me to go back. He in turn told me the little group needed me to teach the class or they'd have to disband. I told Him I'd be missing out on a Bible study I wanted to attend at my new church. Then He hit me with the clincher: 'At this point in your life, it's more important for you to be leading a study than to be attending one.' He wouldn't give up, so I cast the fleece, so to speak. 'Fine, if You have the pastor call me to teach the course, then I'll do it.'

"Wouldn't you know it, the pastor called two days later and asked me to teach the course. That was a miracle in itself because he was extremely upset I had left his church.

"I still didn't want to teach the study, but what could I do? I had to forget about what I wanted to do and undertake what God wanted me to do instead."

When I finished the narration, there was silence on the other end of the phone. "Are you still there, Teddy?"

"Yes. That was a moving story. How long did you teach the class?"

"Three years. Peggy had just started Acts, and I concluded my teaching when we finished the last chapter."

"You spent three years on Acts?'

"I like to be thorough. I could have taught Acts for three more years. It's an amazing book, recounting the early years of spreading the Christian faith."

"I agree, but three years?"

I laughed. "Well, I did bring in other parts of the Bible, and a constant topic of discussion was how God commissions Christians today to advance His kingdom here on earth."

"That makes sense. Did you go on to Romans after Acts?"

"The Lord gave me a signal that my teaching assignment was done. A new member of the class was a Bible scholar more than willing to take over the class, especially if he could continue on with Romans."

8

Friday, December 16, 2011. Something ominous did happen after I completed the last chapter. About mid-afternoon, Molly came running into the office after I screamed "Help!" and fell to the floor. It was what I imagine a sudden heart attack would be like. Only it was my back that had the attack. On a scale of 1 to 10, with 10 being excruciating pain, I was at a 15.

"Paul, Paul, what has happened? Molly cried out as she dropped to the floor beside me.

I pointed to my back and gasped, "The pain, Molly, the pain."

"Let me help you off the floor and into your day bed." How we got there could best be described as pushing a worm from one room to another. She held up my body as I crawled by fits and starts, never in a straight line, from the office to the sun room. That's where my day bed was, a small mechanized hospital cot.

I held on to the edge of the bed with all the strength I had left. An unbroken nausea drenched me; my stomach ached as it had never ached before. I threw up five times in the course of the afternoon and early evening, until all I could do was gag. It was unrelenting. I couldn't make it to my regular bed that night and finally fell asleep through exhaustion about two in the morning. At six I woke up and yelled "Help!" again, and Molly was there within seconds.

"Paul, Paul, is it your back again?" She was half asleep and frantic.

"No, it's the itching. I can't stand it!" The itching was not a new thing, but like the pain, on a scale of 1 to 10, it had risen to a 15. It had never been above a five before, and Molly had controlled it by bathing me with baking soda. She tried that treatment again, but it didn't make a dent. The itching was uncontrollable. I prayed, "Please, Lord, let me die."

"You are going to the emergency room right now," Molly said with the authority of a drill sergeant, as she rushed to the phone.

"Yes, please get me there as fast as you can. I can't take this any longer."

The ambulance arrived in less than ten minutes. The paramedics covered up my head with a blanket when we went outside so I wouldn't chill. Any neighbors watching must have thought they were taking me to the morgue. I was delirious before we reached the hospital and remember very little. But this morning, a week later, I'm wide awake and feel as if I've come out of a long sleep.

When Molly came into the bedroom, she was surprised I was alert. "Welcome home," was the first thing she said after kissing my forehead.

"How long have I slept?"

"Almost a week."

"A week? I can't believe it! It must have been terrible for you, not knowing if I'd ever wake up again. I'm sorry to put you through that."

"Do not be. Remember last week when you said how peaceful I looked asleep?"

"I do, as if it were yesterday. Wait," I said with a grin, "with my being absent in mind for a week, it *was* yesterday."

"You have not lost your humor. I am glad of it. I marveled at how calm your face was. You seemed to be comfortable, without pain or itching."

"What happened after I went off in the ambulance? That's the last thing I remember."

"Well, that is a long story. They wheeled you into an exam room and there was a gastroenterologist waiting for you in blue scrubs. His name was Dr. Smith."

I couldn't help myself with what I said next. "Did he have a beard and a brother next to him chewing cough drops?"

"What are you talking about?" Molly responded.

"You know, Smith Brothers Cough Drops."

"You amaze me. You can find humor anywhere."

"It's the Irish in me. I'll shut up and let you continue with the hospital adventure."

"Dr. Smith had finished a minor operation on another patient. He checked you out and quickly went to a table where a long needle was waiting. I think he knew what the problem was based on the symptoms I gave to the medics on the way in.

He asked me to leave the room, but I refused. "If he dies here, I want to be with him."

"Well, he's not going to die here, but you can stay if you have the stomach for what I'm about to do."

I stayed and soon understood what he meant about having the stomach for it. He took the needle and drained bile from your liver that your diseased pancreas had been blocking. It was awful looking stuff. He said that is what was causing the pain and uncontrollable itching. He also put in a catheter and attached a plastic bag to it, where the bile now drains." Molly said in a voice filled with love, "I now have a new job, emptying the bag."

I reached under the covers and felt the bag. Another something new. The thought of Molly emptying a bag of bile unnerved me. She was too dignified for such an unpleasant task. "There must be something else that happened to cause me to be comatose for a week. Was I given a new medication?"

I'm surprised at how composed and detailed Molly was, as if she were a doctor talking to a patient. "Dr. DeAngelo arrived soon after Dr. Smith finished. I told him about the intensity of your pain. He shook his head and turned to me. 'Paul keeps telling me he wants to go easy on the morphine so he can think clearly. Do you want to continue seeing him tormented like this, unable to focus on anything, holding on to the edge of his bed with white knuckles?'"

"I told him, 'No, I can take no more of his torment. It is killing me.'"

"'Then I'm going to double the dosage,' he declared. Oh, darling, I hope you are not mad at me. It is the morphine that has kept you away for a week."

I sighed. "No, Molly, I'm not mad at you. I couldn't take any more of it either. You made the right decision." With that she collapsed into the chair by the side of the bed. She must have been exhausted staying by my side for a week.

"And look at me, my dear. My mind is as clear as a bell. I'm ready to start writing again."

"I have a surprise for you, darling."

"What kind of a surprise?" I said suspiciously. She held a mirror up to my face and it was a miracle. My eyes were white and my face had lost its yellow pallor.

"The bile backing up is what caused the yellowness. By the way, do you feel any itching?"

"No, that's gone too. Part of the same effect of the bile drainage?"

"Yes."

Although I was lucid again, my body told me I could no longer sit up at my writing table or in front of the computer.

"Molly, my love, can you take on one more job?"

"Of course. What is it?"

"Will you be my secretary and editor?"

"I do not see that as a job. I see it as sharing your life." She hesitated before continuing, "Do you mind if I read the chapters you've already completed?" I had not wanted to burden her with reading and critiquing the story before now. It was to be a final gift when I was gone. I sat up in bed for a few hours watching the news. Much had happened in the week I was gone. Molly checked in several times but didn't say anything.

It surprised me that she read the chapters as quickly as she did, but it shouldn't have. She taught speed reading for many years. When she came back into the bedroom after reading the entire manuscript, she had tears in her eyes. "Was it so hard to read?" I asked.

"It is a wonderful story and gives me hope."

"How?" I asked.

She drew near to me and held my right hand in both of hers. "I realize I will not lose you now. You will be ever present in your memoirs." She breathed in deeply and then let out the air with a sigh, while putting gentle pressure on my hand. Tears ran down my cheeks.

I noticed she had my favorite pen from the office and the yellow legal pad I had used to write the last chapter.

✟ ✟ ✟

2008. I, Molly, am now the transcriber, but not the author, and will portray the story from Paul's point of view.

My story moves ahead to a cold and windy and rainy fall day in 2008. Molly and I pulled out of our garage and drove to the office of a urologist. The purpose of the visit was to hear the results of a prostate biopsy taken two weeks earlier.

The clinic parking lot had only two spots open, both as far from the front door as possible, at least a half-block away. The rain diminished as we stepped out of the car, but the wind tried to blow us into the parked cars we passed.

The urologist's office was in the basement of the clinic, so we took the elevator down and listened to the sound of a motor whirring and a pulley turning. Funny how you remember such mundane things.

When the elevator doors opened, we walked in slow motion to a door with gothic black letters above it proclaiming the word UROLOGY. Five minutes later we were in one of the exam rooms. Molly and I had already talked over possible outcomes, so the room was like a library for ten minutes. Dr. Ferrington entered and we exchanged pleasantries until he looked at the floor and said in a soft voice, "You have cancer." Because I knew my eternal destination, I was distraught but not devastated.

Molly turned into panic mode and gasped, "How long does he have to live?"

"Mrs. Chambers," the doctor answered, "this is at a stage that's very treatable. It's not life threatening."

Molly's demeanor changed from alarm to determination. "What happens now?"

"I recommend taking out his prostate. There are other treatments, but a prostatectomy will give both of you the greatest assurance the cancer won't spread."

"Then that is what we want."

I was the patient but a third-person observer. Molly is not usually pushy, except where my well-being is at stake. I found it amusing. She was like a CEO of a corporation who was making a final decision on bringing in a new product line.

The doctor looked at me for my input. I nodded my head with a smile. Three weeks later I was wheeled into the operating room of a hospital in St. Cloud, forty-five minutes away.

Molly was protective of me as I recuperated and went with me for every follow-up appointment. After the third visit, Dr. Ferrington said the test results indicated my cancer had been contained. What a relief we both felt!

On the way out of the clinic, Molly said, "The news we just heard is exactly what I was pleading with God for."

I responded in a mischievous way. "Well what do you know? God really does answer prayer."

Molly smiled. "Who would have thought it?" Our flippancy lasted the whole way home, a playfulness that had been suspended since I was diagnosed with prostate cancer.

My cancer contained. My life restored. Molly and I able to laugh again. Oh, if that were the end of the story! But it isn't. Cancer is an unpredictable affliction.

9

Wednesday, December 21, 2011. Molly is sitting beside our bed in a new chair she bought yesterday afternoon. It's more comfortable and comes with a snap-on writing table. "I am ready to write. Speak, master, and I will take down every word." We both laughed.

"Molly, you need to stop being a comedian. It hurts to laugh."

"Sorry, darling, my counselor told me humor is good medicine."

"And it is. I was only kidding. Be as funny as you want. I love to see that side of you. Let's continue with the story."

She tried to wear her serious face but was not totally successful. With her legal pad on the table and my pen in her hand, she announced the first line of the new chapter: "It was a dark and stormy night...." I agitated my stomach and back with a guffaw.

✝ ✝ ✝

2009. "OK, let's start there. 'It was a dark and stormy night when my prostate cancer returned in late 2009 and metastasized to other parts of my body.'" Molly smiled and took down my dictation. She knew how this one worked out.

I felt Dr. Ferrington gave me a death sentence, even though he said, "It's slow growing and you will probably die of something else."

"I'm doomed," I said to my friend Neil over lunch.

He replied, "You're not giving a lot of credit to God."

He was right of course. I wasn't trusting in the Lord. Instead of asking for healing, I prayed for comfort and wisdom to live my last days honorably. Who was I to determine what would or would not happen to me? Only God knew the final outcome.

Three days after lunch with Neil, a wave of anxiety swept over me in the early dawn; it took my breath away and threw me out of bed. I ran to the office and pulled out the Bible lying in one of the slots of my roll-top desk. My heart was racing and my mouth was dry. I read chapters 14, 15, and 16 in the gospel of John three times slowly over a period of two hours, letting His words sink into my troubled soul. Eventually, the fear and anxiety abated, replaced by a rustling calm. And in the calm the Holy Spirit gave me a message.

I wrote these words in my journal: "Instead of looking inward with apprehension, experience the majesty of God's creation." Three weeks later the Holy Spirit delivered another critical lesson that cemented my spiritual state of more of God most of the time.

Molly and I visited Hoover Dam during the third week of January 2010 and were perched on top of one of the largest dams in the United States. It made me dizzy to look down.

Hoover Dam straddles the Colorado River and is an astonishing engineering accomplishment, but how it creates electricity is not complex. Lake Mead presses against the walls of the upper dam, ready to let its waters plunge down five-hundred feet to seventeen huge generators below. This is known as potential energy. No real energy is produced until gates are opened and the combination of rushing water and gravity creates an enormous pressure to spin turbine blades and produce electricity.

I spoke to myself – not aloud, to avoid being thought of as loony – this reflection. "If a gate is closed, there is no power. If it's not fully open, the power that generator produces must be diminished. I think there is one gate for each generator. Depending on the power demand, all seventeen generators could be running at once, or only one, or none. "Wow!" I thought. "What a metaphor for the power of the Holy Spirit."

I wanted to jump up and down but didn't for the same reason I chose not to speak my thoughts out loud. When I looked north to Lake Mead, I imagined it represented the Holy Spirit living in my spirit, pressing against the walls of my soul. All that power available to me, but only realized when I opened the gates of my soul.

I shared the Lake Mead metaphor with Molly topside before the two of us took a tour to see the inner workings of the dam. It was a long elevator ride down and a short walk to a large room that looked like a cave. As we gazed over several generators, I turned to Molly and said, "The metaphor I was telling you about continues down here with these turbines. Some are producing electricity because their gates facing Lake Mead topside are open, and some are not spinning because their gates are closed. It's like that with me. I open some gates of my soul to let the Holy Spirit in and keep others closed."

"Give me an example," said Molly.

"My prayer-time gate is usually wide open the first hour of the day, but it starts creeping shut as the day progresses, with all I have to do. I need to keep lifting it up, but I'm not always Johnny-on-the-spot to do so. Life's interruptions are a hindrance."

"So you are the one who decides whether to open or shut a gate?"

"Not quite. I don't choose to lower the gate. It happens when I take my hand off the handle."

"And how do you do that?" asked Molly.

"It usually happens when I pay more attention to what I have to do than to God's plan for my life. I'll give you an example. Ten minutes after my 'Prayer-Time' gate was wide open one morning, an angry client called and accused me of giving her poor advice concerning a meeting that had not gone well. She was way off base. The problem was not what I had suggested she do but what she had done to sabotage the meeting. I was rather rude in my response. My 'Being-Kind' gate had slammed shut."

"But those are two different gates. I do not see one gate influencing another in this dam."

"Sorry. I've stretched out the analogy to more realistically represent my inner workings."

"Is that fair?" asked Molly. "Can you manipulate a metaphor like that?"

"Does it bother you if I do?"

"Well, no, it does not, I guess."

"Then stop complaining." I put on my broadest smile, like an emoji showing I was kidding.

"Ha ha. All right then, twist and turn your metaphor however you want, and I will try to stay with you."

"Fair enough. In the slightly askew illustration, a 'Master' gate influences the other gates of my life. It's called my 'Staying Near the

Holy Spirit' gate, and if that one closes, the others start shutting down."

Molly squinted and put a hand to her face. "This is getting more and more confusing. All these gates opening and closing. You are losing me."

"Sorry; let me try again. Let's say I have seventeen gates within me that control how much Holy Spirit power I allow in my life. Unlike Hoover Dam, some gates are more critical than others. The 'Obeying God', 'Praying Continually', and 'Reading Scripture' gates are three of the more important ones and they influence the other gates."

"This is beginning to make more sense. What are some of the other gates?"

"There's a 'Going to Work' gate and a 'Playing Golf' gate. There are gates for interacting with others and being honest. A tough gate for me to keep open is the 'Patience' gate. There is even a 'Getting Along with My Wife' gate."

Molly laughed with a twinkle in her eye. "You seem to have a lot of trouble with that one."

"I do, I do. Unlike Hoover Dam, the three gates I named have an influence on other gates and other gates have an influence on them. The Lord has told me to love you, but when the 'Obeying God' gate starts to close, my 'Getting Along with My Wife' gate is hard to keep open. When my 'Busyness of Life' gate is letting in the waters of the world, it's hard to open the 'Reading Scripture' gate. Does that make more sense?"

"It does. The open and closed gates are a great illustration of what we need to do on a daily basis to experience the full power of the Holy Spirit. I think of late you have most of your gates open. I need to do better."

"Humble as always. You've managed your gates over the years much better than I have. I sense the image of Hoover Dam is ushering in my final transformation."

"Why do you say that?"

"The sermon in Fargo taught me to listen to the melody of the Holy Spirit that plays underneath the discord of the world and my own self-centeredness. The radio stations vision showed me when I'm in tune with the Holy Spirit and when I'm not. And now the depiction of

Hoover Dam explains how to stay in tune, by opening the gates of my soul to His power."

"But might not the Holy Spirit have another lesson for you in the future?"

"He might, but within my mind I heard a whisper say, 'This is your last lesson.'"

Molly put her hand on my arm. "Thank you for sharing your metaphor."

"You're welcome, but it's not my metaphor. It's the Holy Spirit's metaphor."

10

Wednesday, January 11, 2012. I looked forward to and dreaded the Chambers Christmas get-together of 2011. It would be a time when our family was together for a joyous celebration; it would also be my last Christmas. Jack and his family would be there, and Joe and Celine. I was feeling relatively well for a person dying of pancreatic cancer, almost a 6 on a scale of 1-10. But on December 23rd, I dropped like an elevator in free fall, from the sixth floor down to the basement.

My bile duct catheter became plugged and caused all sorts of problems. I couldn't sleep, eat, or have a bowel movement. Severe pain and nausea overwhelmed me, and the itching was relentless. Dr. Smith was out of the country and couldn't see me until the first week of January. All other gastroenterologists were on vacation or overbooked. Molly told one scheduler this was an emergency. Her reply was, "Ma'am, they're all emergencies."

Dr. Smith was back and available on January 4. I was his first appointment at 8 a.m. "It's well you waited for me instead of letting a non-specialist unplug your catheter. There are other complications I need to take care of."

I was in no shape to ask what the other complications were. An hour later, I was back to normal; that is, normal for a person at my stage of pancreatic cancer. Dr. DeAngelo stopped by the outpatient surgery room at 9 a.m. and increased my morphine dosage a notch or two, sending me back into never-never land.

A week has passed since the unblocking and the morphine increase. I'm feeling better today, in a relative sort of way. If my body were an eight-cylinder car, I'm running on four cylinders instead of one.

Molly came into our bedroom and kissed me on the cheek. My first words were, "I'm sorry I ruined your Christmas," She kissed me again and held my hand.

"You are being too hard on yourself," she said, as she settled in the chair beside our bed with her notepad. "It was a bump in the road, and now you are feeling better."

A raspy laugh came from my throat. "Bump? It was more like a sinkhole in the highway."

"You are funny."

"If I ever lose my sense of humor, I'll be at the bottom of the sinkhole."

"Let us start on the book, if you are up to it."

"I'm up to it. What sentence are we going to start with this time?"

"Call me Ishmael," she said with a devilish smile.

"Moby Dick." It was a game with us over the years. One of us would quote the first line of a book and the other name the book and author, which in this case is Herman Melville.

✞ ✞ ✞

2010. The health gate of my soul was thrown open by Jesus Christ during the first week of December 2010, and His healing power came rushing in. Dr. Ferrington announced that my prostate cancer was in remission. I wanted to jump up and down in his office; and, in fact, did. He took that as a cue to spring out of his chair and put his arms up to signal a touchdown. We both laughed at our foolishness. Molly, who was sitting in the other exam-room chair, was fascinated by our frivolity. She was too proper to dance around like a child, so she just yelled out, "Hooray!"

"How did that happen?" I asked him when we became serious again.

"Your guess is as good as mine. It's unusual for cancer to stop growing when it has metastasized." He hadn't given God enough credit either. "I'd suggest you accept this as the best gift you'll receive this Christmas."

Molly spoke out from her chair. "This is a miraculous Christmas present, a gift from God!"

Dr. Ferrington, a Christian who did not advertise his faith, affirmed Molly's assessment. "Yes, a miracle. That's the best way to describe it." We all bowed our heads in thanksgiving.

Two weeks later my healing gate was still wide open, but my contentment-with-life gate slammed shut. I related the following story to Ben at the coffee shop.

"Molly was out of town staying with our granddaughter last week. I was home alone. I spilled orange juice on my favorite shirt, tossed it in the laundry tub, put in the stopper, and turned on the cold water to fill the tub. Just then the phone rang, and I went into my office to answer it. One of my depression clients was having a meltdown; and in paying full attention to her, I forgot about the running water. Ten minutes later, she quieted down, and I left the office. My first step was into a puddle of water in the hallway. I ran to the laundry room to shut off the water, but it was much too late. A pool of water covered the wooden floors of the hallway and kitchen, ran into the master bathroom, and soaked the living room carpet."

Ben's eyes were open wide. "That's awful." He was about to say more but didn't have the chance.

"I'm not finished. What happened upstairs was nothing compared to what took place downstairs. Water dripped from the ceiling onto the furniture and carpets in the lower level. It was a complete mess. Fear paralyzed me. 'This can't be happening,' I thought. 'Molly will be furious with me.' We recarpeted the lower level six months ago and all the furniture was new as well. I thought how expensive the restoration would be and how much it would disrupt our lives. I didn't know where to start."

"I'm uptight just listenin to the story," acknowledged Ben. "Where did you start?"

"A pile of old towels was in the storage room downstairs, and I used them to soak up the water. That took more than an hour."

"That's the first thing I'd a done, but I'd a used a wet vac from the barn."

"I sold the one we had when we moved into our townhome."

"I'm holdin my breath to hear what you did next."

"You'll find it a bit puzzling, I'm afraid. I sat down in my favorite chair in the sun room."

"You what?"

"After mopping up the floors and wringing out the towels the final time, the enormity of it all hit me. It was a tragedy of cataclysmic proportions."

"What's cattlelistic mean?" asked Ben.

"It's a ten dollar word for disastrous."

"I'd suggest you use lower cost words so as not to lose me. I don't have all your education."

"Sorry, I'll try to do better."

"Good. Go on with your vignette."

"Whoa! Now who's using ten dollar words?"

"Just showin you I'm not entirely stupid."

"Never thought you were." Ben smiled in his trademark smirky way.

"Ok, back to the vignette. My heart pounded like a drum and I gasped for breath. I thought I might be having a heart attack. My chest tightened as if a vice were squeezing me, and my head ached. It was supper time, but I couldn't think about eating. It would be bedtime in a few hours, but how could I ever sleep? And then the next morning…."

"That's when the Holy Spirit entered the picture and told me to sit down and pray. Since I didn't know what else to do, I sat down and prayed. And the more I prayed, the more relaxed I became. He put into my mind a drawing from *The Seven Habits of Highly Effective People* by Stephen Covey." I paused to take a sip of coffee before it became too cold to drink.

"What was the drawing?" asked Ben, now sitting up straight with his hands on the table.

"Give me your pen. I'll draw it on this napkin."

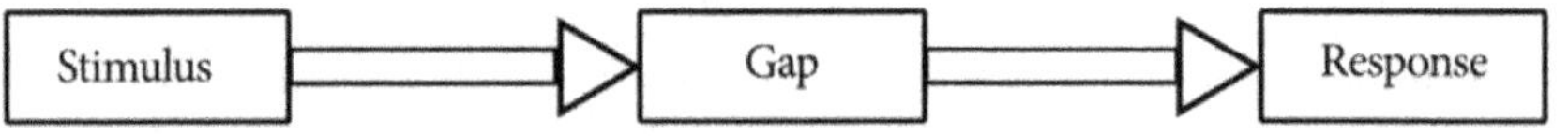

"Covey said we don't need to respond automatically or immediately to a stimulus. We can take a period of time – the gap – to decide how we will react. I didn't have to respond to the townhome disaster with fear and mental paralysis. I could choose a better way. The guidance of the Holy Spirit was the better way. I took a deep breath and said with upraised face, 'I don't have to worry about all this.

You will take care of it in Your own time and in Your own way.' A great calm came over me."

I turned the napkin over and made another drawing. Covey's gap was a secular one of thinking things out before reacting. The Holy Spirit impressed in my imagination a different gap.

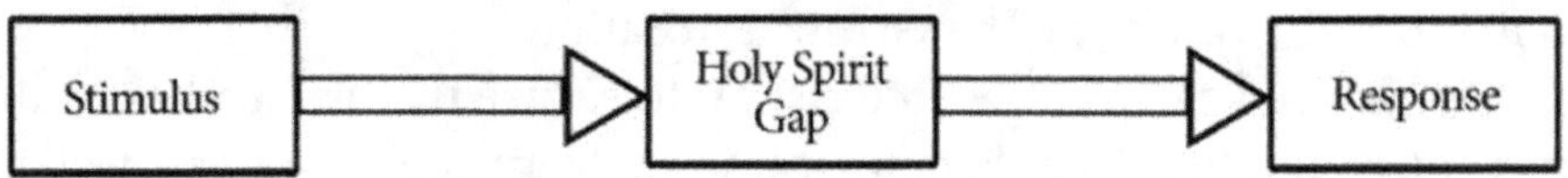

"I'd made a horrible blunder, but it didn't have to define the rest of my life. As I sat passively in the chair, other crises from the past came to mind, in which I survived by the grace of God. I thought of the time I had almost lost my job in college budget cuts, but another administrator unexpectedly left for a better opportunity. And there was a time in my early twenties when a boat I was in overturned in a large lake that had been covered with ice the week before. All I could see were acres of black water and the hint of a light in the far horizon. I feared my time had come, but God miraculously brought me to shore. I wasn't even a Christian then, though He knew I would be one day, which is why I believe He rescued me. If I could trust Him for the then, I could trust Him for the now. I felt at peace, resting in the Holy Spirit Gap.

"I called Molly in Northfield, and she was as upset as a person with such a gentle nature could be. Instead of being defensive, I agreed with everything she said. How could I not? She calmed down quickly, for how do you stay mad at someone who concedes every point? She even started feeling sorry for me.

"An hour later, my youngest son Jack called – the one who's the father of our granddaughter in Northfield. 'Dad, there's a restoration company with an office twenty miles from you that will take care of your water damage as if it never happened. Here's their phone number.' I called and they promised to be there first thing in the morning. I went to bed relaxed, slept well through the night, and awoke with optimism the next morning.

"Our other son Joe called yesterday and suggested I contact our insurance agent. The association insurance deductible was $2,500, but our supplemental townhome owners insurance would cover all but $500 of it."

"That's amazing," Ben said. "You'll have to tell me how it all works out." We went on to discuss other things, including the missionary trip Ben would be taking to Africa the next week to teach sustainable farming to the natives of a small village.

One month later, Ben returned from Africa and called me first thing to get together the next morning – both to talk about his trip and to find out the results of The Great Restoration.

Ben arrived early at the coffee shop to secure the two leather chairs in front of the fireplace. When I came through the doors and walked the eight steps to the fireplace, Ben kidded me. "I raced in from the farm to get these chairs before those two old ladies who sometimes steal them from us showed up. I even bought you a cup of coffee, dark roast with cream and sugar. It's on the table in front of your chair."

"How kind of you," I said with a playful smile, dropping down into the chair reserved for me. "Tell me all about deepest, darkest Africa and how you saved an entire village from starvation."

"That's our second thing," said Ben. "The first is how everything worked out with your townhome do-over."

There was a long pause as I took several sips of coffee while studying my fingernails. Ben was about to protest the silence, but I ended the dramatic delay first. "Marvelously! Absolutely marvelously!

"The restoration company arrived as promised and commenced tearing up floors, setting in fans and dehumidifiers, and otherwise drying up the moisture. In the days that followed, contractors replaced the flooring and repaired and repainted the walls. It was completed a week ago, and you couldn't tell a flood had occurred.

"The restoration had its share of stress: industrial-sized fans roaring like jets on a runway, floors ripped up and new flooring put down, dust abounding, rooms inaccessible, and all the other inconveniences that are part of a major construction project. It was, however, manageable because I chose to place the Holy Spirit Gap between the stimulus of the flood and my response to it. As I look back, I marvel how God took an event threatening to undo me and turned it into a bump in the road. Romans 8:28 once again proved to be true: 'And we know that in all things God works for the good of those who love Him.'"

After concluding the flood story, the agenda turned to Ben's missionary trip to Africa. That discussion lasted two hours.

11

Wednesday, January 25, 2012. Two weeks have passed without Molly and I writing a single word. My day bed has become my permanent abode. I'm in hospice and the oral morphine has been replaced by the drip-drip-drip of an intravenous tube. The sun room looks more like a hospital room. A nurse visits once a day. I'm sleeping more now, which is a blessing; but I want to complete the story. Molly is at my side with writing table down and legal pad ready.

Today is a better day. "Let's give it a try," I say with as much confidence as I can muster. "Let's wrap it up."

"How many chapters do we have left?" Molly asked.

"I have two chapters in mind. That should finish it."

"Two chapters? Let us start on the first one." She put her hand on mine gently and I winced. "I am sorry, Paul. I forgot how sensitive your hands are."

"Don't be sorry. I need your touch; I can bear the pain." She gently cried.

"The past has caught up with the present, Molly. I'm now to the time Dr. DeAngelo told me I had pancreatic cancer, and my health gate slammed shut."

It was her turn to wince. "That was the day my world ended. This will be a difficult chapter to record."

"My world ended that day, also."

"But I am the one who will be left alone." She paused and put on her guilty face. "That is not fair of me. You are the one dying and I am pitying myself."

"You don't need to apologize. You're right. I'll soon be in heaven enjoying myself and you'll be half a person, since the two of us have lived as one."

"I am still ashamed of myself."

"Please don't be. Let's concentrate on the story."

✞ ✞ ✞

2011. In early October of last year, I was in Dr. Ferrington's office for a ten-month checkup to find out if my cancer was still in remission. He had prescribed a CT scan and bloodwork before the visit. Molly was with me.

"The imaging shows something on your pancreas and your complete blood count is not normal." Molly sank in her chair.

I asked in alarm, "Does that mean the prostate cancer is spreading again, and to my pancreas this time?" I had hoped the remission of my cancer would be permanent.

"It's unlikely that prostate cancer would metastasize to the pancreas. We need to perform a biopsy to see what's there."

"And what might be there?" I asked in a quivering voice.

"That's what we'll find out with a biopsy. Let's not get ahead of ourselves until we have all the facts."

Molly didn't say anything until we were in the car. "I am frightened, Paul."

"So am I, Molly."

A week later we were back in the same exam room counting the tiles on the floor. Dr. Ferrington came in with head down and face somber. There was another doctor with him. I had a sinking feeling in my stomach that all was not well. Niceties like, "It sure is sunny out there today," were not advanced. A cloud of gloom permeated the room.

"You're still in remission with your prostate cancer, but the surgeon and pathologist found a malignant mass on your pancreas and spots on your liver. This is Dr. DeAngelo. He'll be taking over your case."

"Why?"

"Because I'm a urologist, and you'll need a pancreatic cancer specialist to properly care for you." The very words pancreatic cancer froze me in my chair. It was a death sentence. Dr. Ferrington saw my dismay and said, "I'm sorry. I'm so very, very sorry."

"How long do I have?"

Dr. DeAngelo answered my question. "I've looked over the results of the biopsy and you're at an advanced stage. I can't say with absolute certainty, but you probably have less than a year to live." He was straightforward but not unkind. His face and eyes showed deep compassion. If I needed a new doctor, he was the one I wanted.

I repeated the words, "I have less than a year to live. How much less?"

"We don't know for sure. Maybe six months to a year. Maybe more than a year. I can't be more precise than that."

Molly passed out in her chair and fell to the floor. The two doctors lifted her up to the exam table and put a blanket over her. She was cold to the touch. I was afraid she might be dead, but her pulse indicated otherwise.

Molly looked up from her writing pad. "How long did I lie there, Paul. We did not talk about it on the way home. Or if we did, I was too distraught to listen."

"A good ten minutes. The doctors had to leave for their next appointments, but a nurse came in and watched over you. You came out of it on your own."

"I neither remember that nor the trip home in the car."

"You were withdrawn for the next week."

"That I remember. I was crushed and in despair."

To that I responded, "Let's return to the story before we get bogged down in unpleasant memories. We're running out of time."

Molly turned her eyes back to her writing pad, pen in hand. "I am ready."

Out of a fog of despair, amidst dark thoughts and self-pity, two words arose in my mind, illuminated as if they were on a lighted billboard during a dark night: REINFORCE RELATIONSHIPS. Underneath the two words was a hierarchical list in a vertical format, one word underneath the other: God, Molly, Family, Friends. Martin Swanson was at the top of the friends list. He led me to Christ in 1982 and served as a Christian mentor until I became a mature Christian.

We started an advertising agency in Willmar, Minnesota a couple of months after my conversion and became business partners, spiritual partners, and best friends. After a year of struggling to earn enough money to feed two families, Martin went back to being an independent artist and I returned to the college from which I had taken a leave of absence. We continued to meet on a weekly basis until Martin took a job sixty-five miles away, after which we met several times a year.

Two weeks after my diagnosis, we met at a restaurant in St. Cloud for lunch. I arrived first. As soon as he sat down, Martin asked, "How are you handling things?"

He had a Bible on the table, as he always did. I thought he'd give me words of encouragement from Scripture, but I should have known better. He wanted to find out how I was doing first. "The week after the disclosure was tough. I shook my fist at God and was angry most of the time. I'm ashamed of being so volatile."

"Don't be ashamed. Job did much the same thing. It's a process. How about this past week?"

"Much better, but I don't feel in tune with God. Do you remember the radio stations metaphor?"

"Of course, and you've been in the upper frequencies experiencing more of God most of the time for, I don't know, maybe ten years or so."

"About that long." I remember having a strange feeling at that point in the conversation, as if we were talking about someone else, a third party I couldn't identify with.

"But I haven't been experiencing God most of the time for the last two weeks. When I need Him the most, I'm farthest from Him. How can I return to most of the time, Martin? How do I get back?"

"Remember, I said it would be a process."

There was frustration in my voice as I replied, "Yes, but I have to start someplace. Where do I start?" I could see tears welling up in his eyes.

His voice cracked as he said, "This is… really hard…Paul." He struggled to compose himself. "I couldn't feel worse if it were a member of my family going through what you are."

"I feel like a member of your family, Martin, ever since the day of my salvation." I tried hard to smile. He was a brother, spiritual partner, and mentor all in one package. His blond hair was barely above his eyes. It had been windy outside, and he didn't take the time to straighten it up when he saw me sitting near the rear of the restaurant.

"All right. Let me try to get through this without blubbering like a baby. Have you ever let the Bible read you?"

"I've not heard that phrase. What does it mean?"

"Let me explain what it means to me," he began. "I believe the Bible is God speaking to me directly and the Holy Spirit exposing the thoughts of my mind, my motivations, my sin, my value, and everything God wants me to know about myself. I believe I cannot know myself without God's voice in Scripture telling me who I am in Christ.

"I had an experience some years back at Alexandria Technical College in one of my commercial art classes. A student accused me of trying to brainwash the class with Christianity. It wasn't true; he was involved in a satanic cult and wanted to take me down. I came within a whisker of being fired. It took a month for the matter to play out. During the first two weeks, I experienced a constant turmoil in my soul and sleepless nights. I was a basket case and could hardly function in the classroom." He paused.

I listened to his story with intense interest. His dark night of the soul mirrored what I had been going through for the last two weeks. "And then what happened?" I asked, hoping it might lead to something that could be of help to me.

"At the end of the first two weeks, I couldn't take it any longer. I wanted to jump in my car and drive down to Texas."

"Why Texas?" I asked.

"Because that was a long, long way from Alexandria. Instead, I did what I should have done from day one. I asked the Lord to show me in His Word a passage that would speak to my soul. He led me to Proverbs 3:24-26, which brought a calm to me every day and every night before I turned off the lights.

> When you lie down, you will not be afraid;
>   when you lie down, your sleep will be sweet.
> Have no fear of sudden disaster
>   or of the ruin that overtakes the wicked,
> for the Lord will be at your side
>   and will keep your foot from being snared

"That Word brought hope to me, as I let the Bible read me. I memorized the three verses and said them over and over and over again whenever I felt anxious. In the end, the college's lawyer suggested to the president that it would be best to drop the charges, which he did. My accuser left the college on the next train to Chicago."

Our order arrived just then and Martin said, "Let's continue this conversation when we're done eating."

While we were eating, I asked the Holy Spirit if there were a verse that could read me in the same way the Proverbs verses read Martin, something that would get me back in tune with Him. He placed in my mind a passage from Jeremiah I had memorized long ago.

> For I know the plans I have for you, declares the Lord, plans to prosper you and not to harm you, plans to give you hope and a future. Then you will call on me and come and pray to me, and I will listen to you. You will seek me and find me when you seek me with all your heart. –Jeremiah 29: 11-13

The food disappeared in ten minutes. After the waitress cleared the table, I disclosed to Martin the verse the Holy Spirit gave me. "But how can pancreatic cancer prosper me and not harm me? How can it give me hope and a future?"

"Let's pray on it," he said.

Martin had taught me a different way of praying that we put in play regarding the verses from Jeremiah. First he'd pray, then I'd pray, then he'd pray – and so on until we discerned we had reached an ending to the subject of the prayer.

On the fourth round, the Holy Spirit gave me the conclusion of the matter. "Oh, Lord, I cannot comprehend how Your plan will give me hope and a future and not harm me. But I don't have to know it; I only have to accept that You have a plan, and it will be good for me."

Martin concluded with, "Paul has seen Your light, Father. He read Your word and was perplexed until he let Your word read him. His future is safe in Your hands. You will never forsake him. I commend his life into Your love and care. In Jesus' name, amen."

As I said goodbye to Martin in the parking lot, my health gate opened up because I knew God was in charge of the rest of my life. I was back in the business of experiencing more of God most of the time.

12

Thursday, February 9, 2012. A lucid mind is not a frequent visitor these days, not after the latest increase in morphine. Dr. DeAngelo said the dosage he's prescribing is pushing the envelope. It's hard for Paul to continue a thought, impossible to complete a chapter. The best he can do is ramble in a muddled and sketchy way and let me sort it out.

"Are you all right with that, Molly?" he asks.

"I am. Together we will make it to the finish line."

I, Molly, am now the narrator and will continue the story as it unfolded in the fall of last year. It is an honor to serve Paul in this way but also an agony to see him in such an altered state. He is no longer the Paul I have shared my life with. He is the Paul who will soon leave this earth for a better life.

"I think this chapter will be the finish line," he chokes out in a hoarse whisper. "There's one more story I want to tell. Beyond that there's nothing more I can think of. Let's try and make it a good one."

I had tears in my eyes and laid my head on his chest while the rest of my body was in the chair by his day bed, the same chair that had been in the bedroom. I held both his hands gingerly because I knew they burned, and he said he felt an infusion of energy from my touch.

"We will make it a good one, my darling. I feel the hand of God on me." With that, I flipped down the desk and sat back to write.

✝ ✝ ✝

2011. Paul and I made last visits during October and November. After that, he was unable to travel. He wants me to relate a visit to Jack's home in Northfield. I remember much of the story. What I did not know, he filled in.

On a Saturday morning in early November, with darkness surrounding the outside of our son's house and darkness within, except for a reading lamp in the upstairs office, Paul read and reread the 3rd verse of Matthew 18. For as many years as I can remember, Paul arose early in the morning and spent the first hour in prayer and Scripture reading. I was careful not to disturb him during that time, unless it was an emergency of some sort. I lifted up my Bible and read the verse to him to make sure it was the one he desired. It was.

"And he said: 'Truly I tell you, unless you change and become like little children, you will never enter the kingdom of heaven.'"

After worship time, Paul went into the bathroom to brush his teeth. He left the door open, as we had agreed, unless he was engaged in private matters. I was right there to observe an awesome scene. Our precious granddaughter walked into the bathroom and put her arms around him and said, "I love you Grampa." Her simple declaration melted his heart.

The next morning we both went to Life 21 Church, where Paul related the episode to the pastor who used it in his sermon. I was sitting alongside Paul in a pew and copied down what the pastor said.

"We need to approach God in the same way Margo loved her grandfather. No analysis. No special circumstances. No hope He will do something for us in return. We are to love Him just because we love Him."

An older woman in the congregation asked the pastor if she could speak. He invited her up and put a microphone in her hand. "As you were telling the story of the granddaughter, an image came into my mind. Jesus was twenty feet high and standing on a flatland. I ran up to Him and wrapped my arms around His leg and proclaimed, 'I love You, Jesus.' He smiled knowingly and put His hand on my head."

"That's beautiful, Maria," Pastor Lew said. "Anyone else have an observation?"

An English professor at one of the two colleges in Northfield came up and took the microphone. "The story of the little girl reminds me of a poem called *The Lamb* by William Blake. The protagonist in the poem addresses a lamb in a pasture and asks in the first stanza who made him. In the second stanza, he tells the lamb that Jesus called Himself a lamb and came to earth as a little child. He concludes with a line that has always moved me: 'I a child and thou a lamb, we are called by His name.'" He stood for a moment as if he were going to say something more but handed the mike over and went to sit down instead.

"We have time for one more," Pastor Lew said.

Before the service, Paul told me about a young woman who came to church with her mother every Sunday but had never come forward for anything. She was mentally handicapped. Her mother brought her up front because she finally had something to say. I will not include her stuttering or hesitancy in speaking. "The story made me think bout a piture I seen in my mind sometime. I'm walkin tward Jesus in a meadow of tall grass and flowers. The wind blows in my face, but not too hard. Jesus is waitin for me with His arms ready to grab me and take me to heaven." Her mother cried as she led her back to their pew. I also cried, as did everyone else.

I looked up from my writing pad and saw Paul was no longer conscious. He wasn't sleeping but had drifted back into the fog from which he had come.

13

Tuesday, March 6, 2012. "Have I been in a coma?" Paul asked as I stepped into the sun room to check on him.

I took a step back in astonishment. Paul had not been clearheaded for a month. He had not uttered a complete sentence in weeks. It was as if Rip Van Winkle had awoken from his twenty-year nap. "Are you really awake?" I asked with a shaken voice. I was suddenly lightheaded.

"It would seem so," he said with a twinkle in his eyes. How could he be whimsical with his second sentence? I guess it should not have surprised me; this was the man I had married. Even facing death, he was amusing.

"I'm wide awake and alert. Why do you find that such a surprise?"

"Because you have been sleeping most of the time and fading in and out of consciousness. The doctor said it was not an actual coma. The only word you uttered in all that time was my name."

Paul laughed, not with a choke or a gasp, but a real laugh. "See, I love you even when I'm unconscious." He sat up and held my hand and signaled that he wanted to give me a kiss on the cheek. I was flabbergasted, delighted, and thankful to the One who gives us life.

"Molly, this morning I can see my life from thirty-thousand feet up in the sky. It's like the Apostle Paul's out-of-body experience. And I can see all the gates of Hoover Dam are wide open."

I am not usually at a loss for words, but this revelation took me by surprise. It was all I could do to say, "What do you see from up there?"

"I see all the threads of my life as one tapestry. Take up your pad and pen and write as fast as you can while I still see it. Don't miss a word, my dear. Don't miss a word."

I bounced back in the chair and proceeded to take down every word. The hospice nurse told me something like this could happen –

one last moment of lucidity before the end. I am happy and sad at the same time.

✝ ✝ ✝

Tuesday, March 6, 2012. "When it's all been said and done, I see my Christian life as three periods of ten years each. The first decade was more of God some of the time. The second, more of God more of the time. And the third, more of God most of the time." He waited until I had written down every word just as he said it and then sat up on his elbows to read the four sentences.

"You have it exactly right."

"I am curious," I said. "Why exactly ten years?"

"It wasn't my timeline, my dear. It was God's. He's the one who saved me in 1982, provided a sermon for me in 1992 in a church in Fargo, and provided me with the interior radio dial vision in 2002. You'd have to ask him why those things happened exactly ten years apart."

He coughed violently and struggled to breathe. "Why don't you give Him a call?" It was a standing joke between us. Whenever I wanted to know God's will in a particular situation, he would say, "Why don't you give Him a call?"

Paul closed his eyes for several minutes. When he opened them, he said, "Where were we?"

I read back to him what I had written so far and then asked a question that had come to me while his eyes were closed. "Could you define each of the ten years by what happened to you during them?" I am not sure if that was really my question or whether the Holy Spirit prompted me to ask it. He kept gathering his thoughts as he dictated his life summary.

"Oh, yes. During the first ten years, I loved God mainly with my mind…in a faith-based way. I'd invited Jesus into my heart…, and He was immediately center stage. But it didn't last.

"After a few months…, I began swapping places with Him. The old me wanted to be the main actor again." He closed his eyes but this time for only a few seconds. "That conflict was the pattern of my life during that first period – Jesus was first, I was first, the world was first – back and forth, back and forth. I wanted more of God in my life on a more consistent basis but didn't know how to get there.

149

"Then came the sermon in Fargo, which started the second period of my life. I began listening for the Holy Spirit more of the time and began following Jesus more closely. If my life were a play, I would be the main headliner in the first period and sharing the spotlight with God in the second. It wasn't until the vision of the radio station dial that He became the permanent headliner, and His final lesson was the Hoover Dam metaphor to show me how to take in His full power. And, oh, the Spirit-filled services and Bible studies I have been to in the last ten years...."

The Lord must have given Paul a huge boost of clarity and energy. He had been speaking haltingly, in short phrases, but with the summation of the three periods of his spiritual life, he expressed himself with a complexity of thought I had not heard for months. It was like Paul of old – articulate, analytical, able to frame a concept with precision and completeness. It was not *like* a miracle. It was a miracle.

He took a moment to collect himself before continuing, which gave me a chance to think about his third period, where he experienced more of God most of the time. He attended what he called Spirit-filled churches whenever he could. It might be when I was out of town for several days caring for Margo. For weekend trips to Northfield when he accompanied me, he always went to Life 21 church, even if he attended an earlier church service with the rest of us first. And every other chance he got. He had a favorite Spirit-filled church in Minneapolis when we visited Joe, which had an earlier service than the one the three of us went to.

I do not know that I can define what a Sprit-filled service is with words, but I certainly knew what it meant when I went with him to one. I prefer churches that are more tame and orderly, like the one in which we are members.

His eyes had been somber during the collect-himself moment but lit up as he continued his thoughts.

"It took me time to experience that degree of passion myself, but I did. I raised my hands during church singing. I went to my knees easily. I praised and worshiped the Lord with all my strength, telling Him over and over again that He was everything to me. I sang with abandon. I cried when He showed me how much He loved me and those around me. I sometimes couldn't control myself. The joy of the

Lord embraced me like a warm mist. I couldn't have imagined such happiness before the last ten years.

"After thirty years in God's classroom, my final degree is at hand." A broad smile came upon his face when he announced with great enthusiasm, "The commencement party is about to begin!"

Those were Paul's last words. He was sitting up when he said them. I do not know where he got the strength. Actually, I do know. From that moment on, he was in and out of consciousness, unable to utter a thought, unable to express feelings, alone in his world of suffering and impending death. I was only an observer.

Epilogue

The day of Paul's commencement party came unannounced. He had instructed me some time back to turn to the November 7, 2011 entry in his spiritual journey for his last words.

"There is no spiritual point of arrival in this present life, no permanent address or inn at the end of the road, no ultimate hook on which to hang our coats. This isn't a world to feel comfortable in. C.S. Lewis captured that reality in *Mere Christianity*: 'If I find in myself desires which nothing in this world can satisfy, the only logical explanation is that I was made for another world.'"

In the early morning of March 15, 2012, my beloved Paul entered a place where there would be more of God all of the time. On his nightstand was the prayer he had written years before and said every night before turning off the light.

> When all is said and all is done,
> When victory over death is won,
> I'll stand before God's precious Son.
>
> I'll gaze into His loving face;
> He'll hold me in His warm embrace
> And whisper words of wondrous grace.
>
> "On earth My music was your song;
> My Spirit made your spirit strong.
> Now dwell in perfect harmony,
> And spend eternity with Me."

www.ingramcontent.com/pod-product-compliance
Lightning Source LLC
Chambersburg PA
CBHW070613120726
47909CB00004B/1208